2/12
w/8/22

SOLITUDE'S LAWMAN

SOLITUDE'S LAWMAN

RAY HOGAN

THORNDIKE
CHIVERS

This Large Print edition is published by Thorndike Press, Waterville, Maine, USA and by AudioGO Ltd, Bath, England.

Thorndike Press, a part of Gale, Cengage Learning.

Copyright © 1988 by Ray Hogan.

The moral right of the author has been asserted.

The text of this Large Print edition is unabridged.

Other aspects of the book may vary from the original edition.

Set in 16 pt. Plantin.

LIBRARY OF CONGRESS CATALOGING-IN-PUBLICATION DATA

Hogan, Ray, 1908–1998.
  Solitude's lawman / by Ray Hogan.
    p. cm. — (Thorndike Press large print western)
    ISBN-13: 978-1-4104-4364-9 (hardcover)
    ISBN-10: 1-4104-4364-7 (hardcover)
    1. Large type books. I. Title.
  PS3558.O3473S6 2011
  813'.54—dc23   2011035070

BRITISH LIBRARY CATALOGUING-IN-PUBLICATION DATA AVAILABLE

Published in 2011 in the U.S. by arrangement with Golden West Literary Agency.

Published in 2012 in the U.K. by arrangement with Golden West Literary Agency.

U.K. Hardcover: 978 1 445 88136 2 (Chivers Large Print)
U.K. Softcover: 978 1 445 88137 9 (Camden Large Print)

Printed in the United States of America
1 2 3 4 5 6 7 15 14 13 12 11

For . . .

My wife, Lois, and our children

CHAPTER 1

Cole Dagget watched the faded eyes of the aged bank teller behind the wire-fronted cage spread and his features pale and stiffen. In the next moment a hard-edged voice coming from the doorway broke the quiet.

"All of you — stand right still and maybe you won't get hurt!"

Dagget swore under his breath. A damned bank robbery! It was just his luck to pick that time to cash the eight-hundred-dollar draft the colonel at Fort Wingate had given him for the bunch of horses he'd just delivered.

"You gents, raise your hands real slow — and they sure better be empty!"

Dagget, clutching the currency he had just received from the teller, endeavored to slip the bills into the cuff of his checked shirt, but failed. As the currency fluttered to the counter and the floor in front of the cage, he swore again.

"Now, turn around and be looking this way so's my partners can keep an eye on you," the man with the calm, unforgiving voice continued. "And you, little lady, just you set yourself down there in that chair by the table and keep out of the way."

In the tense, warm quiet there came the harsh scrape of chair legs on the wooden floor as the girl, who would be Seela Clancy, did as she was directed. Young, no more than fifteen or sixteen, she was blonde and a bit on the plump side, but pretty. Outside in Solitude's only street there was a silence, no passing rigs, no one walking by, no riders coming or going. At that hour of the day, near midafternoon, activity in the small ranching and mining town was at its lowest point.

Cole wheeled slowly. Three men, all masked, were standing just inside the doorway. Each held a gun with its hammer drawn back to full cock, ready to be triggered should it become necessary. One of the trio, a thick, wide-shouldered individual in a dusty dark suit, had a pair of scarred, well-worn saddlebags slung across a shoulder.

"You won't get away with this!" a man standing near the teller said in an outraged voice. Well-dressed in a gray suit, white

8

shirt, and string tie, he evidently was the bank's owner. "We'll have a posse after you before you get a mile from town!"

"Maybe," the squat outlaw replied laconically, taking the saddlebags in his left hand. In long, purposeful strides he moved toward the gate in the railing that separated the lobby area from the bank employees.

Immediately, his two partners — one tall, lean, and in ordinary range clothes, with red hair showing beneath the high-crowned Texas-style hat he wore; the other somewhat younger, also dressed in cowhand gear but with new, elaborately stitched black boots — fell in behind him.

The squat man paused, half turned. He motioned to the younger outlaw with his gun. "Stand by the door, take care of anybody that shows up and aims to come in."

"Sure —"

"Pick up them bills that jasper dropped," he added to the redhead as he pushed through the gate and proceeded to the large iron safe in the center of the room. "Every little bit helps," he added, beginning to stuff packets of currency into the saddlebags.

Dagget drew up stiffly, his eyes on the tall outlaw coming toward him. The eight hundred dollars represented a lot of hard work, as well as signifying better things for him in the future. To lose it meant he could forget about the horses the money would enable him to buy from a rancher up at Mangas Springs who was offering his herd at a bargain price because he was giving up ranching and heading back East.

The horses were already sold at a big profit to the Army at Fort Union. With that money he'd be able to pay off the past-due mortgage on the ranch he'd bought over in east Texas and have a little left over to buy some more stock. Then, having a home base — a ranch with corrals, a barn, sheds, a house, and plenty of water and grass — he'd finally be in business — and in a position to ask Beth Lockhart to marry him.

Some thought his idea of raising horses was bad, that instead he should get in the cattle business. Beef was bringing good prices and the time was coming, some said, when the market for horses would be gone. The government was shutting down forts all over the country, and places like Bayard, Union, Davis, and Whipple would soon be gone, or at best not the good, profitable customers for horses they once were.

That could all be true, Dagget had agreed. Admittedly, a number of Army installations had already been closed, but he figured forts like Union, Whipple, and certain others of similar size, strategically located, would remain active as guardians of the trails for a few years more — five at least. And that would be all he'd need; given a half dozen more deals like the one he'd just made at Wingate and the one he was intending to put through at Fort Union, he'd be in shape to settle down in Texas and start raising a string of fine horses that would bring top prices from the carriage trade.

"That there little gal — she's sure mighty good-looking," the young outlaw said, adjusting his mask in order to see the girl better.

The redhead paused. "You keep your mind set on what you're doing," he warned. "This ain't no time for you to be ogling and thinking about no woman."

"Any time's good for that," the younger man replied in an easy, bantering way. "Yes sir, anytime, anywhere."

The redhead shrugged indifferently. "All right, but that kind of figuring's going to get your head blowed off one of these days," he said, and continued on.

The leader of the outlaws had satisfied himself that he had removed all of the money the safe had to offer and was now crossing behind the teller to get what cash was in the drawer of the cage. Roughly shouldering the teller aside, a graying, chalk-faced man with steel-rimmed spectacles and wearing a threadbare blue serge suit, he began to scoop up the silver and gold coins that were held separate in the cups of a cast-iron muffin pan, and then busied himself collecting the currency that had been neatly arranged on a nearby shelf.

"We doing all right?" the redhead asked.

"Better'n all right," the squat outlaw answered. His voice was filled with satisfaction. "Ain't been doing no counting, but I'm betting I've grabbed up better'n twenty thousand."

"Let's get out of here then. We're pushing our luck taking so much time."

"All right with me. I'm done back here anyway. You ready?"

"Reckon so — soon as I pick up the rest of these greenbacks," the tall outlaw said, and moved in closer to Dagget. "Back up a mite, mister — you're kind of in my way," he added to Cole.

Unreasonable anger surged through Dagget. In a single, flashing instant he could see all his hopes and dreams vanishing like dew under the desert sun.

"The hell with you!" he shouted, and lunged at the outlaw.

As he came up hard against the redhead, he heard the elderly bank teller yell something. A gun blasted, filling the small building with deafening, rebounding echoes and the stinging odor of powder smoke.

The girl screamed, but Cole Dagget was paying no mind to anything other than his own purpose. Seizing the redhead by the front of his shirt Dagget swung him about, then slammed him hard into the counter while he grabbed for the gun on his own hip. His palm closed about the weapon's butt. He started to draw it from the holster — and then everything went black as something cold and hard smashed into the back of his head.

CHAPTER 2

Dagget had ridden into Solitude shortly before noon. It was a warm summer day and, heading the buckskin he was riding into the hitchrack fronting the Bluebird Restaurant, he drew to a halt and swung down from the saddle.

It was his first time in the settlement hunkered against the east side of the Mogollon Mountains like a cornered animal backed against a wall. On to the east he could see the rolling hills and plains country. There were ranches out there, he had been told, while the gold mines were back up in the slopes and the canyons of the Mogollons and the more westerly San Franciscos.

The areas weren't too compatible. The ranching interests looked to the town for one thing, the mining crowd for another, and every now and then a flare-up would occur that caused problems for the law.

But all appeared peaceful now and there

was no hint of trouble as Dagget leaned against the crossbar of the rack and let his eyes course the dusty street. The Bluebird looked to be the only restaurant. Its second floor served as a roominghouse while the Nugget Saloon and Gambling Casino was the principal source of diversion.

Someone named Speakman had a combination feed and harness store. Johnson's Clothing Emporium — Ladies & Gents Ready-to-Wear was fairly imposing as structures went in a town the size of Solitude. Elsewhere along the street were Conroy's General Store & Hardware and Bell's Livery Stable which also housed the local undertaker, one John Counterman.

The Cattleman's & Miner's Bank was in conjunction with the stage depot and was at the far end of the dusty way, and spotting it Cole nodded in satisfaction; he had business to transact there. Dr. Luther Welch maintained his office on the second floor of the Bluebird, and on down the way were more saloons — the Hardrock and the Pick & Shovel.

Well off to one side stood a solitary rock and slanted roof structure bearing the words "Marshal & Jail" above its doorway. At the moment, it appeared to be abandoned, judging by the dense growth of weeds that surrounded it. The only other building visible from the street was a small, clapboard affair painted white on which a cross rising from its peaked roof proclaimed it to be a church.

The houses of the residents were scattered about on the adjacent slopes and flats, some sitting starkly in the open, others graced by trees, bushes, and small garden plots which lent them a more habitable look.

Solitude seemed like a nice, quiet place despite the rumors Dagget had heard in nearby Silvertown concerning the occasional spates of violence, but that was of no concern to him.

He was just passing through. He'd have himself something to eat, maybe visit the Nugget for a drink, and then go to the bank and cash the draft he'd gotten from the colonel at Fort Wingate. That accomplished, he'd ride on. The buckskin was in good shape and he'd stocked up on grub back in Silvertown; thus there was no need to tarry in Solitude, and it was important that he get to Mangas Springs as soon as possible where he expected to buy up more horses for profitable resale.

Pulling himself away from the hitchrack, Dagget had come about, crossed to the Bluebird, and opened the battered, dust-clogged screen door. Entering, he selected one of the half dozen tables placed variously about in the room and seated himself.

A somewhat heavyset, brown-haired, brown-eyed woman, still showing evidence of the beauty from her younger days, came from the partitioned-off kitchen, wiping her hands on a red-and-white-checked apron as she approached. Clad in a calico dress, she looked clean and fresh despite the warmness of the room, and a friendly smile parted her lips.

"Howdy. I'm Lorena Clancy. I own the place. What can I get for you?"

Cole had ordered steak, fried potatoes, biscuits, and coffee, with apple pie to come later, and then leaned back in his chair savoring the quiet of the room, as well as the good, appetizing odors of the cooking food.

"Don't recollect seeing you in town before," Lorena had said a short time later when she brought him coffee and a glass of water. "You just riding through?"

"Yes'm, that's about the size of it," Cole had replied. "Got a little business at the bank to 'tend to, then I'll be moving on."

"Why, my daughter works at the bank — leastwise she does now and then," Lorena said with a big smile. "Her name's Seela —

17

Seela Clancy. She likes bookkeeping, and Aaron Plummer, who owns the bank, is letting her learn what she can there. Doesn't pay her hardly anything, but that doesn't really matter; it's the experience she's getting that counts."

Dagget nodded. Mrs. Clancy was a fine-looking woman, and probably a good cook, but she liked to talk.

"You look like a cowhand," Lorena had continued. "If you're hunting that kind of work, you can probably find it in one of the ranches east of here."

"Not exactly what I do — I buy and sell horses —"

"Oh, I see — a horse trader!"

Cole had shrugged. "Close enough, I reckon."

At that moment a balding, hawk-faced man in overalls and an undershirt and wearing a dirty white apron had limped out of the kitchen and sat down heavily in a nearby chair.

"All done, Mrs. Clancy."

"That's good, Ollie, ought to fix me up for a couple of days, slow as business is." Lorena had paused and nodded at Cole. "This is Ollie. Comes in every other day and washes up dishes and scrubs down the place for me."

"Was a time when I come in every day," the elderly man said. "The mines was all working then."

"That's right. Business certainly isn't what it was a year or two ago," Lorena Clancy had agreed, and then looking toward the kitchen where the sizzle of frying meat was making itself heard, added, "How do you want your steak — still breathing or black?"

"Somewhere around the middle."

Lorena had smiled and moved off. Cole took a swallow of his coffee.

"Just the way I like mine, too," he said, changing to a chair nearer to Dagget. "My whole name's Ollie King," he continued, extending a horny hand.

Cole had acknowledged the introduction and stated his own name.

"Sure mighty pleased to know you," Ollie said. "Heard you saying something to Mrs. Clancy about ranching. Done some cow-punching myself a few years back."

"She didn't get it exactly right. I buy and sell horses."

"A horse trader, eh?"

Cole had stirred. Getting people to under-stand the distinction between the two seemed to be an impossibility. He had never liked the title much, believing that it didn't fit since he did no trading, but confined his activities to buying and selling. However, he never allowed the difference to cause him any loss of sleep.

"Ain't many horses around here that a fellow could buy. A few mules, maybe."

"I've never had much to do with them."

"You're being smart!" King had said. "Contrary damn critters. Only way you can get one to do what you're awanting done is to hit him over the head with a two-by-four and get his attention. Maybe then he'll listen to you. I recollect once up at Gold Creek, a camp north of here, I —"

"You been around here long?" Cole asked, anxious to head off a tedious, rambling yarn.

"About twenty years. Was here quite a spell before Harry Brinkman and John Clancy — Mrs. Clancy's husband — come along. Seen them out slaving on their claim many a time." Ollie had leaned forward and with lowered voice said, "That was before they busted up. Was over Mrs. Clancy — she was Lorena Cartright then. Worked in the Nugget. A dance hall girl. Had a little daughter of her own from a earlier marriage."

Dagget was staring out of the window at the distant flats. Somewhere a dog was barking — the only sound to be heard other than Lorena Clancy bustling about in her kitchen as she prepared Dagget's meal.

"Clancy and this Brinkman do all right mining gold?"

"Yeah, finally hit it big, but it didn't last long with Clancy — leastwise till he teamed up with Lorena. She sort of settled him down. Brinkman was different. Could say he sure wasn't under the table when brains was being passed out. Took his money and bought a lot of land east of here and went into the cattle business — somebody said he'd once been a rancher over Texas way."

"He get out of mining altogether?"

"Nope. Done right good at ranching, but he was smart enough to grab onto a couple of claims that keep paying off. Hired three or four men to work them for him."

"He still hang around here?"

"Sure," King had replied. "Here and Silvertown, and now and then makes a trip to there and maybe on to Lordsburg. The main bank's got its office in Lordsburg."

"Anything wrong with the bank here?"

"Nothing," Ollie King said, shifting on his chair. "Well, it ain't exactly a real bank like a man might expect. Folks just sort of bring their gold to Plummer — he owns the place — to be picked up and hauled to the stagecoach to Silvertown or on to Lordsburg.

"Of course the merchants here deal with

21

Plummer, but the big reason he stays open is to handle the bullion from the mines and to take care of their payroll."

The room had filled with the odors of steak frying, potatoes, and browning biscuits. Dagget, finishing his cup of coffee, stirred in anticipation. The meal should be about ready. He turned again to Ollie King.

"You said Brinkman and Clancy split up over Mrs. Clancy. Why?"

"Hell, they both wanted her — she was really something to look at in those days; still is, I reckon. Happened she picked Johnny — John. He was a laughing, smiling sort of a man, always happy. Guess you could say he still is. Folks took to him like ticks to a deer. Never knowed an enemy, that man. Now Brinkman's different. Real quiet and always all business. Got that no-nonsense way about him.

"But don't go getting me wrong. Harry's a mighty fine fellow. Little hard to know and he's good to them that works for him — and he's honest as the day is long."

"He ever marry after losing out to Clancy?"

"Nope, never did. I've seen him setting with different gals at the Nugget and then maybe going off to their rooms now and then, but he never got interested serious like with no other woman after —"

"All ready," Lorena's voice cut Ollie's words short.

Cole pushed back his chair as the woman placed the platter of food before him. That done, she smiled at him. "You're needing more coffee."

As she hurried off toward the kitchen, Ollie had risen. Offering his hand, he said, "Was a real pleasure meeting you, Dagget. I'm hoping you have good luck in your horse trading."

Cole had nodded, shook the older man's hand, and then, picking up his knife and fork, began to eat.

The meal was delicious and satisfying. Lorena Clancy brought in more crisply fried potatoes and kept hot biscuits, butter, and honey ready to eat while seeing to it that he never lacked for coffee. When he finished, he thanked Lorena Clancy, paid the dollar-and-a-half check, and returned to the street.

For a time, he stood in front of the restaurant enjoying its shade and the taste of the fine dinner Lorena Clancy had provided. The street was still deserted and lounging against the front of the building, Dagget was having a few more moments of ease before he went on about his trade. A fairly tall man of twenty-five or so, he was of wiry build, although muscular, had dark hair and eyes, and a hard-set mouth overhung by a full mustache. Dressed in tan pants of some hard, finished material, he was also wearing a red-and-black plaid shirt, leather vest, yellow neckerchief, and knee-high boots with blunted army spurs. A black, flat-crowned hat that showed much weathering was on his head, a Colt .45 hung on his right hip, while on the left, a long, keen-bladed Green River knife was sheathed.

Finally stirring, he had pulled away from the building, and freeing the buckskin, had swung into the saddle. Coming about, he headed for the bank at the upper end of the street. He'd get the draft cashed, put the currency he'd received in his money belt, and set out for Mangas Springs. He could cover a few miles before dark and it got time to make camp.

CHAPTER 3

Cole Dagget came back to consciousness with a dull, aching pain in his head. He lay quiet, vaguely aware of shadowy figures moving about him, of many voices, some angry, others excited, filling his ears.

"He's coming to —" The words seemed to come from a distance.

Cole stirred and managed, with the help of someone, to sit up. All about him were the sounds of confusion and the sharp tang of powder smoke still hung in the warm air.

"I reckon he ain't hurt bad —"

"That redheaded jasper sure walloped him a good one with his six-shooter —"

"Yeah. Sure too bad old Lester weren't that lucky."

Cole's head was clearing rapidly and his senses were back almost to normal, although dulled by a throbbing pain.

"Who?" he asked, struggling to rise. He glanced at the doorway where three men were carrying out a body.

"Lester — Lester Zale, the teller," a man nearby replied. "One of them outlaws shot him dead. Guess Lester was trying to stop him from getting away with the money. That's Lester them fellows are carrying off to the undertaker's now."

The portly, well-dressed man Cole had assumed was banker Aaron Plummer looked up from the desk where he was counting a small amount of coins and currency. "Looks like they got away with about thirty thousand dollars. Won't exactly know until —"

"The hell with the money!" a harsh voice cut in. "They've got my girl — took her hostage. I'm getting up a posse right now."

That would be John Clancy, Dagget realized, his attention switching to the speaker. Middle-aged, squat, with clear blue eyes and dark hair, Clancy contorted his ruddy features with worry.

"Did somebody go after my wife?" Clancy continued in a high, ragged voice. "I got to tell her so's —"

"Probably knows by now," someone said, his words barely audible above the hubbub. "Stacy's woman went to tell her."

"How much money did you lose?" a woman standing next to Dagget asked. "Somebody said you had just cashed a draft or something."

"Eight hundred dollars."

"I guess you could say you got off easy."

Cole swore under his breath. It was an appreciable fortune to him and represented all the cash money he had in the world, except for a small amount of change in his pocket. Buying up the horses he'd just sold to the Army at Fort Wingate had taken all but a few dollars of his capital, and losing the eight hundred meant he'd be right down to scratch again and forced to start over.

All of which meant his hopes of marrying Beth Lockhart, as well as his dream of settling down on the ranch in Texas and raising fine horses, would have to wait a while longer — unless he could do something about recovering his stolen money.

"What about the posse?" Clancy demanded.

"Sure, John — everything's being taken care of. Just takes a little time to saddle up the horses and for the men to get ready. Harry Brinkman's sort of heading up things."

"Brinkman!" Clancy shouted angrily. "Why the hell him?"

"Seemed to be the only man around with enough sense to get things organized. Now, if we had a lawman —"

"Ain't there a lawman here?" Cole asked, surprise and disappointment in his voice. "Saw a jail —"

"We used to have a marshal." It was Ollie King, the swamper from the restaurant. "Quit about a year ago and we ain't been able to hire one since."

Dagget frowned as he gently rubbed the side of his head where the outlaw had struck him. "Understood a lot of gold and payroll's handled here. I can't see how —"

"The stagecoach carries two shotgun riders. They look after any shipment once they've taken charge," Plummer explained, coming into the conversation. "I have responsibility for the gold when it is brought in for shipping to Silvertown, generally for only one day. The payroll's different. It's sent up from Lordsburg. The outlaws got it and the cash I keep on hand."

"They take only currency?"

"Currency and the gold eagles. Guess they didn't want to be weighed down with silver."

Lorena Clancy burst into the room and pushed her way through the crowd to her husband. Her ashen face was streaked by tears and torn with worry.

Clutching Clancy by the shoulders, she cried, "Is it so? Did some outlaws take Seela — kidnap her?"

John nodded woodenly and endeavored to take the woman in his arms. She pulled away from him and turned to the others in the hushed room.

"That's my daughter, my little girl they've taken!" she said in a quivering voice. "God only knows what they'll do to her! Won't some of you do something?"

"We are, Lorena," a tall man who had just come through the doorway said. "I'm getting horses — seven of them. All I need now are men to ride them."

This would be Harry Brinkman, Cole reckoned. Tall, also in his forties, he was a lean, square-jawed man with dark eyes and hair, and a cool, quiet way. Dressed in a gray suit, white shirt, string tie, wide-brimmed hat, and boots, he had a gun belted about his middle and a rifle hanging loosely in the crook of his left elbow.

"I'm calling for volunteers," he said, raising his voice. "Need six men."

"Five," John Clancy amended. "You don't think for one damned minute that I won't be going! She's my daughter, and I sure ain't too old to set in a saddle."

Brinkman merely shrugged, his gaze reaching out over the room, and he nodded as he chose the men he wanted from among those volunteering. His eyes halted when they came to Lorena Clancy. The words, "Don't worry," formed soundlessly on his lips.

"All right, you men that are riding, get your gear and meet me at Bell's in fifteen minutes. Horses will be saddled and bridled and ready to go by then."

"Fifteen minutes!" Lorena muttered bitterly. "They'll be miles from here by then with the start they've got."

"Chance they'll drop her off when they get to the forks," someone suggested. "One of the outlaws had her riding double with him."

"That's right," one of the volunteers chosen to ride in the posse said as he and the others moved toward the doorway. "Be too much of a load on a horse if the fellow riding him was in a hurry. Slow him down plenty."

"I don't know — Seela's not very big," Lorena said doubtfully.

"Just leave it to us, Lorena," one of the riders said reassuringly. "We'll bring her back . . . anybody know for sure which way they went?"

"North — took the road to the forks. Probably headed east for Socorro when they got there."

"And they could've swung left onto the

Escondido Trail for the high country. That'd make more sense."

"Yeah. Maybe it would, but I expect Brinkman'll figure what to do when we get there — and it'll be right. He has the knack of always knowing what to do."

Cole had worked his way slowly through the crowd to the door. His head still ached, but he was thinking clearly. One thing was certain in his mind — he was glad the outlaw had used his weapon as a club and not triggered it as the one behind the counter had done. He guessed he was too close to the tall redhead to permit a shot. He'd had one bit of luck there.

"Ain't you riding with the posse?" a man asked.

Cole shook his head. Too much time had already been lost and he could see no point in waiting for Brinkman and the others. They would not be ready for at least another quarter hour — perhaps longer.

"No, figure I can save time by heading out after them myself."

"I see — sort of taking on the job as Solitude's lawman."

"Reckon you could say that," Dagget replied, and stepped out into the afternoon's warm sunshine.

The outlaws, it was said, had headed

north with the girl, Seela Clancy, and the money — his money. Riding alone, he could cut down the lead they had, possibly even get them in sight before the posse ever got well started.

CHAPTER 4

Farther down the street, Cole could see three members of the posse sitting on their horses in front of Bell's Livery Stable patiently awaiting the remainder of the party. He had little faith in the possible accomplishments of such a gathering. Posses, as a rule, failed in what they undertook, particularly if the chase lasted for any length of time.

Members, enthusiastic at the beginning, usually tired and, feeling the need for warm food, a good bed, and family companionship if they were married men, ordinarily were all too ready to turn back after a day or two in the saddle.

He felt sorry for Seela Clancy just as he did for her mother, Lorena, and for her father who seemed genuinely worried and distraught by her abduction. He hoped, as someone had suggested, that the girl had been abandoned somewhere along the way.

Cole had his doubts there, however. The outlaw who had been guarding the door had been far too interested in Seela to release her until he was finished with what he evidently had in mind.

Dagget reached the hitchrack at the side of the bank. People were still hanging around the building, wandering in and out, milling about in the street as if relishing the details of the shooting and abduction, as well as the robbery.

Jerking the buckskin's lines free, Dagget gathered them into his left hand, and grasping the horn with his right, swung up into the saddle. At once the horse began to move off, eager to get on the trail once more.

The buckskin was a perfect specimen, having a tawny gray, short, husky body with a black mane and lower legs. A gelding now, he was among the first bunch of mustangs Cole had trapped. He had made up his mind to get in the horse business one day when he was working cattle in Nevada. Mustangs were running wild all through the hilly area where he had camped, and it had come to him that here was a natural and possibly inexhaustible source that would enable him to supply the needs of the Army who seemed always in the market for good horseflesh.

Persuading two cowhand drifters to work for him after promising to pay them top wages as soon as he made his first sale, he set up shop in an abandoned homestead, the owner of which was unknown. Making good use of a nearby dead-end canyon, he and his helpers soon had a fair-sized herd in the corral they had thrown together. Culling out thirty or so of the best, they began the job of breaking them to leather after releasing the unsuitable ones. Of the lot selected, the buckskin was the prime animal, and taking great pains with his training, Cole had turned him into an excellent trail horse.

Dagget held the gelding to a fast lope for the first few miles and then gradually slacked off. He hoped to find Seela Clancy somewhere along the well-marked road, but there was no sign of her — which he more or less expected.

A short time later, he came to a small stream and, fording it, drew to a halt on its far side. Dismounting, he allowed the buckskin to catch his breath while he searched about for the three sets of hoofprints that would assure him that he was on the right trail. They were not difficult to find in the rich, dark soil, softened by a rain shower that had fallen earlier that day.

Satisfied, Dagget climbed back into the saddle and resumed the trail. It would fork when it veered nearer to the pine-studded mountains, one leg going on to the settlement of Socorro lying along the Rio Grande to the east, the other climbing up into the higher regions of the towering San Franciscos, the western chain of the Mogollon Range, he remembered having been told.

It would have been pleasant riding along the cool, winding road thickly bordered by tall pines, musky-smelling junipers, and various clumps of scrub growth, had not the loss of his money weighed so heavily on his mind. The losing of his entire capital of eight hundred dollars which had taken so much time, so many hours of sweaty, backbreaking labor to accumulate was a blow to his future — one that would take months to overcome.

Thinking of the money, Dagget urged the buckskin to a faster pace. He could see now that it was going to be up to him to overtake the outlaws and recover the cash without the help of the posse.

A twinge of guilt seized Cole Dagget. He realized he was thinking of his money first and the safety and well-being of Seela Clancy second. Suppose Beth fell into the hands of outlaws such as the ones he was pursuing; what would he think of a man who could have helped her, but for some personal reason did not?

Dagget shook his head. He reckoned he was so intent on his own problem and thoughts of the future that he was overlooking the most important thing — the girl! Well, that wasn't the way it would be; if he found the outlaws first, he'd have it out with them, free Seela, and then recover the stolen money. After that, he'd wait for the posse to arrive, turn the girl and the bank's money over to them, and ride on.

He was glad of one thing — that he didn't have his packhorse. The bay he used whenever a lengthy trip was ahead of him was as good a horse as could be found, but regardless, leading a pack animal always slowed a man down considerably, and the way this trip had turned out, he needed all the speed he could get out of the buckskin without running him into the ground.

The road now began to curve to the east and Cole reckoned he was not far from the fork someone had spoken of. He began to speculate on which route the outlaws had taken as the buckskin loped steadily along. If they had distance in mind, they would no doubt keep right and continue on to Socorro, the main road used by stagecoaches, wagons, and pilgrims heading west. If they intended to go into hiding, they likely would cut back up into the high mountains where there were probably countless side trails and numberless empty cabins abandoned by disheartened miners who had given up all hope of ever discovering gold and becoming rich. The latter choice seemed more logical to Dagget, but he would not guess; he'd wait and see which way the tracks of the outlaws' horses went when they reached the fork.

A long-eared mule deer bolted across the road suddenly, causing the buckskin to shy. There was a lot of game in the country, Cole had been told — deer, squirrel, rabbit, wild turkey, and numberless quail and doves. If he were not in such a pressing hurry to reach Mangas Springs and conclude the deal for horses — and he got his money back — it would be nice to pull up somewhere in the forested hills, camp, and do a bit of hunting.

It would be a fine place to live, he mused, but not a very practical one for raising horses. His ranch in the Monument Hill country of Texas where a fair-sized creek cut away from the Colorado River and bordered along its edge, was to his thinking the ideal location for what he had in mind.

The slopes of the short hills were covered with grass rather than rock and there was always plenty of water supplied by the river or the frequent rains that refreshed the land and kept it green. Dagget hoped he'd be in a position to move to the ranch and start raising horses soon, but at the moment, unless he could recover his money, that day appeared to be well off in the future.

Near dark, he came to the fork in the road. The hoofprints of the horses the outlaws rode were too indistinct to see from the saddle despite the soft ground, and, drawing to a halt, Cole got down to make a close examination.

He walked slowly up the fork that led to Socorro, but failed to find any evidence that the three horses had passed that way. There were only the day or so old wheel prints of a stagecoach drawn by a six-up, and the wider, flat tracks of a heavy wagon of some sort.

But this did not necessarily mean the outlaws had chosen to head up into the mountains. They could have struck out across country, taking no specific trail but making their own way through the oak brush and trees toward some particular destination that they had had in mind when planning the bank robbery.

He'd soon find out if that were the case, Dagget thought as he doubled back to where he'd left the buckskin; he hoped this wasn't true. The outlaws could have struck out in a dozen different directions and tracking them alone would be impossible.

Reaching the split in the road, eyes urgently straining to pick up the outlaws' tracks in the closing darkness, Cole turned onto the trail that angled up the side of the mountain. It was not wide enough for a wagon or for two men on horseback to ride side by side.

A dozen slow steps and Dagget came to a stop. A patch of reddish soil softened by a small creek which strayed randomly down the slope provided the evidence he needed. In the fading light were the hoofprints of two horses walking shoulder to shoulder while a third, apparently following a short distance behind, left its marks between them. There could be no question; the outlaws were heading for the high country. Wheeling about, a hard, satisfied smile on his lips, Dagget hurried back to the waiting buckskin.

Thrusting a foot into the stirrup, he started to mount, but paused as a thought came to him. The posse would wonder, too, which fork in the road the outlaws had taken and much valuable time would be lost as they endeavored to puzzle it out.

Ground reining the gelding again, Cole hunted up a wrist-size stick and, sharpening one end with his knife, dropped back to the main road and drew a line in the soil starting on the road and curving left onto the mountain trail the outlaws had taken. He grooved the mark deep enough so that anyone off his saddle and searching for tracks would be certain to see it. However, to make doubly sure, Dagget backtracked to the road and, at the point where he had started the groove, drove the stick upright into the ground where it could not possibly be overlooked by the posse.

That accomplished, Cole trotted back to the buckskin, mounted, and started up the trail. The growing sense of urgency that now gripped him was tempered only by the fact that it was near dark and necessary to halt periodically, dismount, and examine the soil to be certain the outlaws were still ahead of him, a necessity that gradually began to occur with greater frequency as night closed in.

A time later — two hours or so — and not long after he had forded a small creek and made one of these stops, Cole Dagget swore deeply as he carefully searched the trail. The outlaws were no longer somewhere in front of him. They had turned off.

Chapter 5

Cutting his horse about, angry at himself for his carelessness, Cole began to backtrack along the trail. It wouldn't be long before trailing the outlaws by their tracks would be impossible since light was failing rapidly. He knew he must find the prints of their horses before that time came, or give up the hunt until morning.

Dagget located the tracks a yard or so above the creek that angled across the trail. The outlaws had waded their horses through the shallow water and then, moving off the path, headed south into the trees and brush covering the steep mountainside.

Cole gently pulled off his hat and ran fingers through his hair as he gave that thought. His head no longer pained him, but there was a tenderness in the area where the outlaw had struck him. Why would the killers swing off an easily traveled trail, along which they could move fast, and strike a course across the side of the mountain — a route that certainly would be very difficult and much slower? It could only be that they were heading for Arizona and were familiar with a different route. That had to be it.

At once, Dagget left the trail and followed. It was fairly easy at first to see the hoof-prints of the three horses as the rain had softened the soil, but as the minutes wore on and darkness increased, it became necessary to rely on broken branches and occasional halts while he struck a match and made certain the tracks were still ahead of him.

He wished now he had taken time to set up a marker at the point where the outlaws had turned off the trail, as he had at the fork in the main road, so that the posse could continue on the right track, but it had not occurred to him and he was reluctant now to take the time to double back and correct the oversight. But likely Harry Brinkman, who seemed to have assumed charge of the party, had a good tracker on the job and —

A rider, hunched low in his saddle, burst suddenly from the brush to Cole's left. The gun in his hand blossomed bright orange fire, and Dagget felt the shock of a bullet as it seared across his arm.

Instinctively, he swerved off into the shadows, and spurring the buckskin, rushed deeper into the dense growth covering the mountainside. It had been one of the outlaws — the tall redhead who had knocked him unconscious in the bank. They had spotted him trailing them, had laid an ambush and, like some greenhorn, he had ridden right into it.

But he had been lucky. The bullet had inflicted only a minor wound in the fleshy part of his arm, and while he could feel blood seeping from it, he knew the injury would not handicap him to any great extent.

He slowed the buckskin's headlong flight, half turned, and listened into the hush. There were no sounds of the outlaw pursuing him. Evidently the redhead thought his bullet had done a better job and there was no need to press the ambush further.

Pulling to a stop, Cole continued to listen for signs of the outlaw's presence and, finally convinced the redhead was nowhere around, came off the saddle and began to care for his wound. Using some of the disinfectant salve that he always carried in his saddlebags for such injuries, he applied a thin coating to the wound after which he took a strip of white cotton cloth that had once been a shirt and bandaged the area.

That done, Dagget climbed back into the saddle and, fearful of losing the outlaws, rode quickly and quietly back to where he had encountered the redhead.

The killers would continue southward across the mountain, he supposed, if they were intending to go into Arizona or some other point in that direction. When he reached the place where the outlaw had taken a shot at him, Cole dismounted and, again using matches, located their trail. At once he resumed following, but his efforts were short-lived. The tracks on the leaf- and needle-strewn trail ended abruptly.

Hindered by the darkness and rapidly running out of matches, Dagget searched along both sides of the path but could find no sign of the riders continuing south. And then it occurred to him that he may have been following a false trail — that the outlaws, discovering him on their heels, had intentionally turned south, suckering him into the ambush. Now convinced they were rid of him, they had turned about and were doubling back to the main trail. Reversing his own course, Dagget slowly backtracked along the path. A short time later he straightened up; he was right — there were hoofprints of three horses leading back across the mountain's slope.

Immediately, Cole got back into the saddle. Guiding the buckskin off to one side of the path in the event the outlaws might be watching him, he struck a parallel course for the main trail. He hadn't been far from it, he realized a short time later when he came in sight of the creek that crossed the trail, and veering toward it, but keeping well within the shadows of the pines, he came to a halt and listened for anything that would tell him the outlaws were nearby.

Somewhere a night bird called into the soft darkness and far off in the direction of Socorro, coyotes were setting up a discordant chorus. Other than those, there was nothing but the stillness of the hills. The moon, struggling earlier to make itself known, had now broken free of the clouds and was shining brightly, illuminating the slopes with a silver glow and creating deep shadows in the hollows and among the trees.

There were no signs of the outlaws. Cole, riding in close, checked thoroughly above and below the creek's crossing and, finding no hoofprints, turned back to the path that the outlaws had made. He found the tracks where they had approached the trail — and there had disappeared. Cole considered that puzzle for several moments and then came to a conclusion; there could be but one explanation — the outlaws had ridden into the creek and were effectively hiding all signs of their passage by keeping their horses in the water.

Sooner or later they would come out of the creek, Dagget reasoned, and at that point he could trail them again, assuming the moon stayed out and did not again become obscured by clouds.

Reasoning thus, Dagget started upstream, allowing the buckskin to walk along the upper side of the stream. Odds were good the outlaws would head for the higher regions of the San Franciscos, he figured, when they decided it was safe to pull out of the creek.

Dagget took comfort from the fact that the outlaws were still carrying his money since they had not halted anywhere after leaving Solitude. He hoped Seela Clancy was all right, too. That the outlaws had no intentions of leaving her anywhere along the trail had become apparent since the fork. He recalled then what the young outlaw said about the girl back in the bank — words that promised only a time of terror for her once the party had halted and made camp for the night.

He wished the posse would show up, but there was still no indication of them anywhere. Undoubtedly the party was somewhere on the side of the mountain by that hour. Again, Cole regretted he had left no marker at the place where the stream crossed the trail that would direct their course.

Facing a light breeze out of the north, Dagget pressed on. An owl searching for prey swished by on near silent wings, curious about his presence. The coyotes were still at it and likely would be for the remainder of the night. Cole continued, walking the buckskin as fast as he could while keeping an eye on the banks of the small creek as it followed a slightly winding course across the mountain.

After a time, the creek began to widen and grow deeper and Dagget reckoned he was getting close to its source — a spring most likely somewhere above a ledge that he could see looming gradually in the higher distance.

Dagget drew up sharply. Ahead, a wet spray on the rocks bordering the stream drew his attention. Dismounting, Cole crouched beside the darker wetness. Fresh hoofprints in the ground a step or so beyond the stream's bank told him what he wanted to know; the outlaws had cut away from the creek and were taking a direct course up the slope.

This would slow them down considerably, Dagget reasoned, and his chances for overtaking them now had improved greatly. Cole smiled tightly at the optimistic thought. It would be true if he could find their trail. The slope was overgrown with brush and looked to have many stretches of rocks and loose shale. Even with a new bright moon, it would be difficult to pick up the tracks of the horses.

Leading the buckskin, Dagget started up the slope, the tracks of the outlaws' mounts visible to him, but shortly, when he reached a wide outcrop of granite, he lost all sign of the animals. The outlaws had apparently guided them around the glazed, slanting sheet of rock as it would have been impossible for the horses to climb up or move across it — but which end had they chosen to circle?

Dagget could find no clue on the hard, rocky ground and, after giving it thought, decided the north end of the hard mass would be most logical. Accordingly, he got back into the saddle and began to make his slow, tedious way along the base of the huge granite slab. Twice the buckskin slipped on the slanting surface and after the second time, Cole dismounted and led the gelding.

He continued on that course for a good

half mile and then came to a halt. A sheer wall of rock faced him. It was a dead end — he had chosen the wrong direction. The outlaws, evidently familiar with the area, had turned south.

Cursing his luck, Dagget got the buckskin turned around and started back over the course he had just covered. When, once again footing for his horse was secure, he mounted and crossed to the opposite end of the slab which gradually was turning into the base of a steep escarpment. But there was a trail to follow, one made by deer and other animals, and, at once, Dagget swung onto it.

An hour later it ended on a rocky hogback, again leaving no indication which way the outlaws had taken — to the right, to the left, or on ahead through a tumult of weather-smoothed rocks.

Dagget sighed wearily. There seemed no end to the problems that faced him. That he had managed to draw near the outlaws was evident, but once again he was at a point where to guess was the only answer if —

The faint tang of woodsmoke coming in on the slight breeze brought Dagget about. A campfire — off to the north. It could be the outlaws halted for the night, or it could be a miner or a cowhand, possibly even a drifter. Whatever, he had no choice but to determine which.

CHAPTER 6

"That's the stage a-coming!" John Clancy called to no one in particular in the posse. "Running late."

The party, after finally getting under way, was a mile or so below the fork. Conscious of the fading daylight and the inevitable arrival of darkness, they had ridden hard since leaving Solitude.

"Pull up!" Harry Brinkman, who was slightly ahead of the other riders, yelled, raising his hand. "Want to talk to the driver." And as the posse came to a halt, he added, "Could be him or the shotgun rider saw the outlaws — or some sign of them."

"It'd be a real fine thing if they came across Lorena and John's daughter standing in the road and picked her up," Ed Speakman said, easing back in his saddle. "We could call off this here hunting party then."

"You're forgetting the money them outlaws got away with," Dave Contor reminded him. "Had all I've got stashed away in Plummer's bank. Ain't sure I'll ever see any of it again unless we can catch that bunch."

Both Clancy and Brinkman rode forward a few paces and, with hands raised and palms forward, gestured for the coach to stop. The mud-spattered vehicle with its six-horse hitch came to a creaking, chain-rattling halt, the back wheels locking and skidding as the jehu, an elderly, bearded man with black, shoe-button eyes hauled back on the lines and stood on the brake.

"What the hell you jaspers doing?" he began as the guard lowered his rifle and settled back. "Thought for a bit we was being held up."

"Dan, did you pick up my girl somewheres along the road?" Clancy asked in an anxious voice as he rode in close to the stage for a look inside.

"Nope, John — and I ain't got no passengers either," the driver replied. "What's this here all about anyway?"

"Three men held up the bank —" Brinkman began.

"Was four of them," Clancy interrupted. "Held up Aaron Plummer, kidnapped my girl. Got away with thirty thousand dollars. Was three of them that done the robbing, but they had another jasper in the bank at the time. Was sort of a lookout — or maybe we ought to say a rear guard."

"Three or four — it don't matter much," Brinkman said angrily. "Point is did you see any sign of them along the road?"

Dan stroked his cropped beard. He was seemingly more interested in watching several piñon jays busily engaged in stripping a small juniper of its berries than in answering Brinkman's question, but finally he shook his head.

"Nope, I ain't seen nobody, leastwise not on the road. Ain't saying they couldn't've been off in the brush. If they was, they stayed out of sight."

The shotgun stirred and squared himself on the seat. "I sure didn't see nobody either, Mr. Brinkman."

"Nope, I reckon you didn't," the old driver said dryly. "You been asleep ever since we left Frisco Crossing."

"The hell I was! I was only resting my eyes and —"

The remainder of the posse had moved up and was clustered about the coach. Dan nodded briefly to those he knew and turned his attention to Clancy. More jays had joined those in the juniper and their noisy quarreling was disturbing the horses.

"Mighty sorry to hear that about your girl,

Johnny. Wish I could tell you I'd seen them bastards that took her so's you could get right after them, but I sure didn't."

"I was hoping they'd drop her off some-where along the road after they got out of town — but I can see now they didn't."

There was a long minute of silence broken only by the quarreling jays and the move-ments of the restless coach horses. Brink-man shifted in his saddle.

"We better keep going," he said. "Longer we stall around the farther away they'll get."

"I reckon you're right," the old driver said, kicking off the brake and gathering up the lines. "Good luck."

"Obliged," Harry Brinkman said, nod-ding.

"Much obliged," Clancy also said, as if Brinkman's reply was not sufficient or in order. "I'll appreciate your telling my wife that you seen us when you get to town — and that we ain't found Seela yet."

"I'll tell her," Dan said as the horses lunged into their harness and the coach whirled away.

"Which way we going?" Jim Fontane, one of the posse riders, asked, shifting his gaze from the departing vehicle to Brinkman. "Ain't hardly no use of us following out the Socorro road."

"Just might be at that," Brinkman answered, frowning. "Dan said they could've been off in the brush hiding, waiting for the stage to pass."

"Yeah, maybe so," Fontane said as the posse moved on toward the fork.

"Could split up. Two men, at least, could go have a look," Conroy said. "If they seen them or signs of them, one could stay and the other come back for the rest of the posse."

"Sign — what sign?" Ed Speakman demanded scornfully. "That coach and them six horses pulling it will have tromped out any sign of them on the road."

"Conroy's got a good idea," Brinkman said. "Might spot them on up the road and —"

"I'm again' that," Clancy broke in, "be wasting two men. If that bunch was on the Socorro road, Dan or that shotgun rider would have seen some sign of them. Four men with my girl riding double with one sure couldn't keep out of sight easy."

"Maybe so," Ben Wilk, riding alongside Fontane, said doubtfully, "but I've been through there many a time. They's lots of brush and trees, big rocks, too. Hiding would be mighty easy."

"I'm inclined to agree with Ben," Speakman said. "He's been all over these hills doing his mining. Expect he knows what he's talking about."

"Yeah," Conroy agreed. "Ben ought to know what he's talking about . . . John, you still think that fellow Dagget — I think Ollie King called him — is in with them other three outlaws?"

Clancy pulled off his hat and wiped at his forehead with the back of his hand. In the afternoon sunlight his hair had a thick, dark look that contrasted with the blue of his eyes and enhanced his strong, handsome face. It wasn't hard to understand why Lorena had chosen him over the more staid, ordinary-looking Brinkman.

"I sure as hell do. He was right there in the middle of it all!" Clancy said.

"Could've just happened he was there at the time," Conroy said. "He was cashing a draft or something, I heard, and if he was one of them, he took a pretty good wallop on the head."

"Expect that was all for show —"

"Hell, John, that don't make much sense. Why would they have him doing that?"

"That ain't hard to figure out. He was there to keep an eye on things, hang around for a bit afterward, and see what the town would do. Could be he was hoping for a chance to lead a posse off in the wrong direction."

"Well, he sure didn't do none of that," Pete Odle commented dryly. "Soon as he got his brains back from that knock on the head, he climbed on his horse and took out after them others."

"Which sort of proves my point, don't it?" John Clancy said. "He was wanting to catch up with the rest of his bunch. He weren't about to let them get too far ahead with his share of the money."

"That's all pretty thin," Brinkman said. "Can even say farfetched."

"The hell it is!" Clancy shot back angrily, his features reddening. "What makes you think you're always so damn right!"

"One of these days them two are going to have it out for good — and I'm hoping I won't be around close," Conroy said to Jim Fontane in a low voice, and then to break the sudden tension, added, "Which way we going, Harry? We're coming to the forks."

"Don't be asking him!" Clancy snapped before Brinkman could reply. "We'll head up the mountain — follow the old Escondido Trail."

"Could be that's what we ought to do," Fontane said mildly. "Howsomever, I figure somebody ought to ride up the Socorro road for a ways, don't you think so, Harry?"

Brinkman had pulled to a halt in the center of the road. "Can maybe handle it another way," he said, and beckoned to Odle. "Pete, have a look at the trail heading up into the hills. See if there's any tracks."

Fontane smiled in satisfaction as the slim cowhand, one of Brinkman's employees and known as an expert tracker, swung from his saddle and began to examine the narrow road climbing up into the mountains.

"If they all went up the Escondido, Pete'll know it right quick," the rancher said. "Can depend on it."

"We're wasting time," Clancy said impatiently, sawing his horse about. "They had to go this way —"

"Best we be sure, John," Speakman, a tall, lean man hunched over on his mount, said placatingly. "Won't pay to get halfway to the top of the mountain or most of the way to Socorro and find out we took the wrong road."

"We won't be making no mistake," Clancy declared. "They didn't head for Socorro — we already know that!"

"Just don't know for sure," Brinkman said wearily. "We're all just aiming to make certain we're right."

"You ain't running this posse, damn it!"

Clancy yelled. "And I say we move on without wasting no more time. It's my girl that the renegades've got!"

"Know that, John, but if we make a mistake and don't find that bunch before — well, before they hurt her, it'll be dogging our minds for the rest of our lives . . . Any luck yet, Pete?"

Odle was a good ten yards up the Escondido Trail. He paused and turned half around. "Ain't nothing that I can see so far. I'm starting to look on the shoulders."

"Well, hurry it up!" Clancy said in a loud voice. "It ain't like we've got all day. Going to be dark here pretty soon," he added to the men near him. "Why don't we all start looking?"

"No need," Brinkman said quickly. "Could mess things up for Pete — and if anybody can find sign, it'll be Pete."

"Him not finding any could mean that bunch did line out for Socorro," Ed Speakman said.

Dave Conroy struck a match to the half-smoked cigar clamped between his teeth and nodded. "I'm beginning to think Harry's idea of us splitting up, half heading for Socorro and the rest going on up the Escondido Trail's a good idea."

"Sounds good to me, too," Fontane

61

agreed. "We could figure up a signal of some kind — two quick shots for whichever bunch of us finds tracks or spots them so's the others could join up."

"Now, that's right smart and —"

"Reckon here's the tracks, Mr. Brinkman," Pete Odle called.

At once the posse hurried forward and ascended the trail a short distance to where the cowhand was standing.

"They went and done just what I had a hunch they'd do," Pete said as the riders halted before him. "Rode along the shoulder for a spell — all except one —"

"That'd be that Dagget catching up," Clancy said.

"And then they turned back onto the trail — all four sets of tracks are going up onto the mountain."

"Just what I figured," Clancy said triumphantly. "Hell's fire! We wasted a whole half hour setting around jawing about it! Let's get moving."

"Go ahead, lead the way, John," Speakman said. "You were right all along."

"We best let Pete take the lead," Brinkman said as Odle mounted. "We can follow two abreast — trail looks pretty narrow."

"Why does Pete have to go ahead?" Clancy

demanded angrily. "Ain't no doubt we're —"

"I want him to keep a close eye on the tracks just in case those outlaws turn off before we spot them," Brinkman said coolly.

"That's a good plan," Fontane said, pulling his horse back to let Odle pass. Others in the party murmured agreement to the arrangement.

Clancy shrugged and nodded reluctantly. "All right, just so we don't go too damn slow. Already lost too much time."

CHAPTER 7

Dagget rode slowly off the hogback in the bright moonlight, continued on down a fire-scarred, barren slope, and halted by a small stream. The smell of smoke was stronger in the arroyo-slashed swale along which the creek cut its course, and reasoning that whoever had built the fire would have chosen a site for a camp along the water, Dagget began carefully and quietly making his way upstream.

It could be the outlaws, and again he wished the posse would put in its appearance. He didn't know what he would do with the girl, assuming he had now overtaken the outlaws and was successful in a showdown with them. That was all he really cared about — recovering his eight hundred dollars, riding on to Mangas Springs, and closing the deal for the horses that had brought him into that part of the country in the first place. One thing he knew for certain, the rancher was eager to sell out and wouldn't hold off for him indefinitely.

Buying up the rancher's remuda and driving it back to the forty acres in Texas's Fayette County would be the final step in getting into the horse-raising business right. It seemed long ago that he had set his mind to that purpose, and bearing in mind advice his father had given him, he had never permitted anything or anybody to alter his course.

However, if he failed to recover his money or get to Mangas Springs in time, he would face a serious setback — one that could take him years to recover from.

He had already made plans for the Mangas Springs herd; the horses the rancher had to sell were all good stock, he'd been told, and there was no reason to doubt that. Once his, he'd cull the choice mares, breed them to the fine stallion he already had, and sell the rest to the Army. His dream would be reality then — just as would be a life with Beth Lockhart.

Several mule deer, having come in for their day's end watering, looked up, startled at the sudden, quiet appearance of the buckskin rounding a bend in the creek. Immediately they threw back their heads and rushed off into the trees, their hasty departure, in turn, frightening a half dozen ducks paddling about in a small backwater of the stream.

Cole halted. In the cool quiet the fleeing deer could have been heard by anyone close, and he had no idea how near he was to the campfire. Slumped in the saddle, he waited out a long five minutes. When there was no indication of anyone having taken note of the deer's flight, he moved on.

The smell of piñon smoke was now stronger in the air, but he had yet failed to catch sight of a fire. The outlaws, if that's who it was, had built their camp in a place well hidden from view to most directions. He was a mile or so from the trail, he reckoned, and a blaze as small as this apparently was would most certainly go unnoticed by anyone in passing. It had been by sheer luck that while halted on a rocky hogback, he had caught the odor of smoke.

Cole pressed on at a faster pace, aided by the bright moonlight that flowed across the slopes and flats. Several times he paused to look back on the direction of the trail, hopeful of seeing some indication of the posse or hearing an encouraging sound — but each time was a failure. He could not really expect anything else, Cole told himself; he was too far off the trail for the posse to be following unless, by pure luck, they picked up his tracks and those of the outlaws.

He failed, too, in his efforts to detect any noise that would indicate he was drawing near the fire and what he hoped was the outlaw camp. There was no doubt that it was ahead — and not too distant. The good, tangy smell of burning piñon wood, and the fact that he was still following along the stream made this a certainty.

He was still troubled by what he would or could do with Seela Clancy once he had disposed of the three outlaws. That latter condition had not presented itself with any force to him earlier, but now he began to consider it. He would be up against three hardcase outlaws who would not hesitate to kill him if he gave them the opportunity.

That he was better than average with the six-gun he carried on his hip could not be denied, but the outlaws also would be expert, possibly even better, and it would be foolhardy to think he could face all three at once in a shoot-out. The odds would be overwhelming and chances were he'd never come out alive. It would be a matter of outsmarting them in some way, just how, he'd not know until he overtook them. Perhaps following the timeworn, but effective, strategy of divide and conquer would be the answer.

The wailing of the coyotes had increased as the moon strengthened and now seemed to be coming from the nearby slopes instead of in the distance. Wolves, too, were making their presence known but to a much lesser degree than their distant kin, thanks to the efforts of ranchers who continually hunted the larger doglike animals because they preyed on the young of their livestock. Miners, too, sought the great gray and brown lobos for their hides which were considered quite a trophy.

"Been right so far, ain't I?"

The harsh words coming out of the night brought Cole Dagget to a quick stop. A slight wind had risen in the east, and the smell of woodsmoke now came from that direction.

"Yeah, I reckon so, but —"

Dagget came off the buckskin swiftly and quietly led the gelding to one side where he tethered him to a small pine. He could not be certain the voices, coming from the opposite side of a brushy weed and rock-studded mound directly ahead, were those of the outlaws he was trailing. The only way to know for sure was to move around through the undergrowth to where he could see them.

"Was right about this here place, too, weren't I? No chance of a damn posse coming up the trail, spotting us."

All doubt in Cole Dagget's mind vanished with those words. It was the outlaws — otherwise there would have been no mention of a posse. Drawing his gun, Cole began to work his way through the brush and rocks on the east side of the mound, taking each step with extreme care. If the killers heard him and made the first move, he knew he would be in deep trouble.

"Was right about that bank, too. I recollect you didn't want to believe me when I said there'd be a pile of money there just waiting to be took. And there weren't no law dog either, just like I —"

"Sure, Jube, you had it figured good all along. Got to hand it to you." The voice of the second outlaw was familiar. It would be that of the tall redhead. "Point is how long are we going to lay around here?" There was impatience in the man's tone.

"Long as I figure it'll take. Sure don't want to show ourselves till we're damn sure there ain't nobody around looking for us."

"Ain't much chance of that," the redhead said. "We're plenty far from the Escondido."

"Way I wanted it, Mister Apache Reed," Jube said, pride still riding high in his voice.

"My ma never raised no idiot when she brung me up, ain't that right?"

"Reckon so, Jube," Reed admitted patiently.

Dagget, dropping flat, began worming his way slowly through the knee-high weeds and grama grass. Reaching a shallow dip, he paused, removed his hat, and cautiously lifted his head.

The two outlaws were hunched by the fire. A blackened coffee pot was on the ground nearby along with a quart-size bottle of whiskey. As Cole watched, Jube shifted the flour sack draped across one knee to the side, and taking up the liquor, poured a quantity into the cup of steaming coffee that he held. Just beyond them were two horses. They were picketed close to the stream where they were grazing on the short grass growing along its banks.

Where was the third outlaw? Where was Seela Clancy? There was no sign of the girl or the swaggering, young outlaw, and only two horses were to be seen. Had they ridden on?

It would be easy to handle Reed and Jube as they sat by the fire unsuspecting he or anyone else was even remotely near, but making a move against them without knowing where the third bank robber was could be a fatal mistake. He would have to know before he did anything.

Keeping low, Cole resumed his tedious way through the weeds, waist-high at that point. The grama no longer was present, crowded out by the hardy weeds which now made it possible for Dagget to make his stealthy approach on his knees.

Suddenly a dry branch cracked under his weight. As Cole sank deeper into the rank growth, Apache Reed came to his feet.

"You hear that?" he demanded. "There's somebody out there!"

"I didn't hear nothing," Jube said, pouring himself more coffee and again lacing it with whiskey.

"It was something —"

Taut, gun in hand if it became necessary to use it before he made certain of the third outlaw's whereabouts, Cole rode out the tense moments.

"You're as jumpy as an old woman," Jube said, taking a swallow from his cup. "Was a deer, like as not. Couldn't be nothing else. Sure'n hell ain't none of them counterjumpers that'd be in a posse. A man could never get them off the trail into rough country like this!"

Reed nodded and slowly settled down on the flat rock he was using as a seat. "Yeah, expect you're right. Where'd Cooter go?"

Jube jerked a thumb over his shoulder at the area farther around the rocky mound. "Over there somewheres wrassling with that gal, trying to make her see things his way."

"Hell, he's been doing that ever since we left town —"

Relief slipped through Dagget. He couldn't see the young outlaw, whose name apparently was Cooter, but from what Jube had said and the offhand gesture he'd made, the missing man and the girl were farther to the left along the weedy mound. Likely the third horse was close by, too. But Cole Dagget had never been one to take anything for granted on such critical occasions; it paid to know for certain, he had learned, and again, keeping low, resumed a slow, careful circuit of the outlaws' camp.

Reed was uneasy, that was apparent to Dagget as he worked his way slowly to where he could see the west side of the mound. Jube had called the redhead "Apache." It could be the man had some Indian blood in his veins and such was making him more alert to danger. The redhead continually looked over his shoulder into the direction where Cole had broken the dry branch underfoot.

Cole halted and raised his head slightly

above the weeds for a better look into the shadows on the west side of the mound. He smiled tightly. Cooter was there — just as Jube had said. The outlaw was hunched on his heels apparently facing Seela. Dagget could not see the girl as she was hidden behind a clump of brush.

It would be necessary to move forward a few more yards to see if Seela Clancy was all right. However, he would be limited there as the tall weeds ended short of the creek, leaving only open ground. Taking a cautious look at Apache Reed and the outlaw leader, Jube, and seeing that they had not changed positions, Cole began to make his way toward Cooter. After he had covered what would amount to a long stride, he paused and, again, raised his head. He could see the girl.

Seela, hands bound behind her back, was sitting with her shoulders against a large rock on the side of the high mound. Her head was lowered and Dagget could hear her sobbing raggedly.

CHAPTER 8

As near as he could tell, Seela had suffered no mistreatment so far — she was probably more frightened than anything else. She did show the effects of the outlaws' hurried flight, however; the hem of the dress she wore was torn, and dust streaked her skin and dulled her blonde hair. She appeared to sag from weariness. That it had been an ordeal riding double with the young outlaw, Cooter, was evident.

If the posse arrived now, the girl would be little worse for the experience, but there seemed little likelihood of that. If there was a good tracker in the party, which was a reasonable assumption, and he had puzzled out the hoofprints of the horses where the stream had crossed the trail, there was then a possibility the riders would come.

"Like I done said, I can be real nice to a pretty young gal like you." Cooter's voice was low and insistent.

Seela raised her head slightly. "My — my pa will kill you," she said brokenly.

Cooter laughed. "Your pa? You see him around here somewheres? You sure don't — and you sure won't because he ain't got no idea where we are. Old Jube Fowler took care of that. He knows this country like a parson knows his Scriptures. He picked this here spot because he knew nobody'd ever come this way."

"He — they'll find us," Seela promised stubbornly. "You'll see — and if you even touch me, Pa'll see that you're strung up —"

Again, the outlaw laughed. "I ain't afeared of him, honey, or none of the rest of that posse because, come morning, me and you're pulling out. Jake and Apache are for leaving you right here, letting you get back to that town best way you can — if you can."

"Oh, please — do that!" Seela cried, her voice brightening. "I can walk back — I'm used to walking!"

"You're a far piece from the trail, then it's a mighty long ways to that town. I got my doubts you —"

"I could make it —"

"Well, you won't have to fret none about it. I told Jube and Apache I'd taken a fancy to you and aimed to take you right along

75

with me."

Seela Clancy began to weep again, her shoulders shaking visibly from the sobbing. "I — I want — to go home."

"Now, you best stop that bawling," Cooter snapped, his tone hardening. "It won't do you a mite of good. From now on, you're my woman, and you'll keep right on being my woman no matter what."

Tense, crouched low in the weeds, Dagget listened to the exchange between the girl and the outlaw. Impatience shook him. He was wasting time, he should be making his move. Cole gave that thought. He would like to help the girl, relieve her mind, but for a moment she would be all right — and to jump Cooter would create a disturbance and bring Apache Reed and Jube Fowler down on him fast. It would be wiser to drop back, take care of the two older outlaws first and then turn his attention to Cooter. The odds would then be more in his favor.

Carefully turning about, Dagget began to double back to the outlaw camp. He had no plan in mind how he would handle the two men, but he knew it must be done singly and quickly. A gunshot or any other indication of an encounter would summon Cooter and he needed to be ready when he faced him.

"Well, I for damn sure ain't never going to let them lock me up in a cell again —"

It was Jube's voice. Dagget raised his head slightly and looked about. He was now opposite the two men hunkered by the fire. Cooter and the girl were no longer visible to him as they were now hidden by the end of the high mound.

"Never was put in no real pen," Reed said. "Was locked up in a jail a couple of times."

"Lucky," Jube said. "Had me three years in the Texas pen, and five more over in Yuma. Made a break there. Give the guards a slip one day by jumping into the river and hiding under a boat that was heading downstream. Near drowned."

As Dagget continued to work his way through the weeds, the outlaw hawked and spat into the fire.

"Hell of a place to get sent — Yuma," he continued. "If ever some judge sentences you to there, you'll be smart to first grab a gun and blow your head off."

"Been told it's a mighty mean place — hotter'n the gates to hell, and that the guards are the meanest that ever drawed a breath."

"Can bank on it. Know for damned sure they'll never get me back there alive — or any other pen far as that's concerned." Jube

77

paused, patted the flour sack hung across his leg. "With my share of the money in this here grub sack, I'm lighting out for Mexico."

"Figuring on doing that myself," Reed said, tossing the last of the wood that was piled nearby into the fire. "You wanting some company?"

"Sure thing," Fowler said. "Soon as it's morning, I aim to cut back through the mountains for Arizona, then head south for the border. Ain't much between here and there but hills and open country — and no towns. When a man gets to the Pedregosas he's most there. Some mountains — about twenty, maybe twenty-five miles from the border."

"Sounds good to me," Reed said, rising. "Expect I'd best get us some more firewood. Long time till morning . . . When you aiming to divvy up the money?"

Cole, lying quietly in the deep weeds, began to work his way forward to a stand of oak brush and pine trees a dozen strides off to his left. If he could catch Apache Reed away from the camp where he could deal with him alone, the situation would quickly simplify.

"In the morning, I reckon, when we get ready to pull out," Jube replied, pouring himself a drink from the bottle. The coffee pot was evidently dry and the two outlaws were now treating themselves to whiskey in a cup.

"I figure this here'll be my last go-around, and I aim to make the most of it when I get to Mexico."

"You think it'll be all that easy getting there?"

"Sure. Might have to do a little seesawing back and forth along the New Mexico-Arizona border, but that won't be no problem. Don't worry none — we'll make it all right."

Reed was still standing at the edge of the fire's glow, his expedition to get more wood postponed for the moment.

"I ain't exactly worried," he said. "Figured a long time ago that I was living on borrowed time. But now, getting all that money kind of changes things."

"Sure does. Makes a man feel right good to be heading for Mexico with his poke full of greenbacks and double eagles — and don't be carrying it in your saddlebags. Like I said before, that's the first place a law dog'll look if he figures you been up to something. Stow it in your grub sack, like I done, or maybe carry the greenbacks in your boots."

Reed swore deeply. "A law dog or any

other man'll have one hell of a time taking my share away from me. Ain't never seen that much money, much less had it . . . Any special place in Mexico we'll be heading for? Ain't never been there."

Dagget had reached the heavy brush and, moving cautiously, drew himself upright. Apache Reed had taken a pipe from his pocket and was tamping tobacco from a pouch into its bowl. The coyotes and the wolves had quieted and the only sound at the moment was the distant hooting of an owl.

Cole was hoping luck would be with him, that Reed would come his way in search of wood. If it worked out as he wanted, he could then confront the tall redhead, get him out of the picture, and then take on Fowler. If all went well, he could get the outlaw leader out of the way in time to have a showdown with Cooter.

"There's a lot of little towns across the border where a man can bed down and live high on the hog if he's got hisself a stake. And it ain't far to Chihuahua — that's a real big town if a man's of a mind to go where there's a lot of folks. Some mighty fine parlor houses there, too."

"Just getting across the border'll suit me," Reed said, striking a match to his pipe. He puffed the briar into life and then moved off into the moonlight-shadowed night.

Dagget hunched lower in the darkness of the brush and trees. It would be no trouble to open fire on both of the outlaws from where he was hiding, but that would shift the advantage to Cooter who, thus forewarned, could duck into the cover of the weeds and trees and have a choice shot at him.

No, best he follow the plan that he had in mind, Cole decided, and that was ambush Reed, knock him out with the butt of his .45, and then handle Jube Fowler in the same manner. It would be simple, once Apache was out of the way, to slip up behind the outlaw leader, knock him senseless also, and then take care of Cooter — so busy trying to convince Seela Clancy to see things his way to be aware of what was happening.

Cole drew up slowly. Apache Reed had changed directions; he was not heading for the deep brush. Instead, the outlaw was veering off to the right toward a fallen tree that evidently offered a good supply of dry wood.

Immediately Dagget began to move off through the silver-shot darkness. He should be able to reach the dead pine about the time the redhead had finished collecting an armload of wood and was starting back to the camp — but he would have to hurry. Everything depended upon his taking care of Reed without Jube or Cooter becoming aware of it.

Hunched low, moving in and out of the brush and trees as fast as possible without creating any untoward noise, Dagget continued to circle the outlaw camp. If he should —

"Hold it right there, mister!"

CHAPTER 9

"There's a whole mess of tracks around here, Mister Brinkman," Odle said, holding the lantern he had brought along close to the moist ground so that its light could reveal the hoofprints of the outlaws' horses. The posse had halted on the Escondido Trail where a small creek tumbling down from higher regions cut a shallow channel across the narrow path. "Seem to me heading back, mostly south."

"South!" John Clancy echoed. "That don't make sense."

"See if you can follow them out, Pete," Brinkman said, ignoring Clancy's loud comment. "Could be a trick to throw us off," he added as the cowhand moved off.

"They would've had to stay on the trail," Clancy insisted. "Country on both sides of us is hard going."

"You're right, John." Speakman said. "Hunted deer up here a couple of times.

83

It's plenty rough."

Brinkman, gray hat tipped low over his eyes, let his glance touch the members of the posse, some smoking pipes or cigars, some slouched in their saddles, one off his horse and stretching his tired muscles. Of them all, he reckoned Pete Odle was the only one that it could be said he was close to — and that possibly was due to the fact that Pete was on his ranch payroll.

Conroy, Speakman, Wilk, Jim Fontane — he knew them all well and had for many years, but it ended there. They fell far short of what could be termed good friends. They treated him coolly, respectfully, and with a slight hostility as if he instilled a measure of fear within them.

He had been told once by one of the girls at the Nugget, whom he visited occasionally, that he was not good at making friends and certainly the opposite of John Clancy, who had but to walk into a room filled with strangers and emerge in a short time on a first-name basis with them all. Brinkman had wished often that he had a different personality, but there seemed no way to change, and he had continued to live his life the only way he knew how.

The wealth that had come to him from the partnership with Clancy in their gold mine, and subsequent investment in cattle and other interests, had somehow removed him even further from the acquaintances he'd made over the years and, he had thought often, had cost him Lorena.

When Clancy and he had met Lorena, they were on more or less equal footing insofar as riches were concerned. Both had courted her but his becoming involved in ranching and other investments had absorbed his spare time which left the field open to John Clancy. And Clancy, with his smiling, winning personality, had made the most of it — possibly not intentionally taking advantage of the situation, but certainly bringing an eventual end to their longtime friendship and winning the hand of Lorena as well.

Now they were enemies — just why Harry Brinkman was unsure. Perhaps Clancy resented his continuing success and steady accumulation of wealth and power while his own fortunes had declined sharply. The gold mine had petered out and investments in several others had proven unprofitable, leaving him almost broke. In fact, the restaurant he had purchased for Lorena while he was riding high, and at her insistence someone had said, was all he had left now of a once sizable fortune.

Knowing how Clancy felt about him, Brinkman likely would have passed up riding with the posse had he not felt he owed it to Lorena to do all he could toward getting her daughter out of the hands of the outlaws and seeing her safely home.

He hoped there would be no confrontation with John Clancy, but having lived and worked with the hot-headed Irishman for years, and knowing him well, Brinkman realized that this was likely to occur, if not in the coming hours while the posse searched for the girl, then on some future date. Clancy seemed always on the prod and ready to turn a simple meeting into a serious confrontation for no good reason at all.

For Lorena's sake, he would do all he could to avoid a showdown, for he realized killing Clancy in a brawl or a shoot-out would only hurt her while doing nothing to alleviate the deep loneliness he had felt for Lorena since losing her. She was the only woman he had ever loved and wanted for his wife — but he had lost her and nothing could ever change that.

"Where the hell did Odle go?"

Clancy's peevish question brought Harry Brinkman's thoughts back to the moment.

"If he ain't back here in a couple of more minutes, I say we move on — keep going up the trail."

"No way to be sure them outlaws went that way," Ben Wilk said hesitantly. "Need to know for sure. Just could be they lit out across country."

"Or headed back south into the mountains like them tracks say they did," Fontane added. "What do you think, Harry?"

Brinkman shrugged. Reaching into his inside coat pocket, he produced a cigar. "I say we stay right here until Odle gets back. Be fools to go rushing off blind in country like this," he said, biting off the closed end of his smoke and lighting the weed with a match.

"The hell you say!" John Clancy shouted, swinging his horse around to where he faced Brinkman. "I'm going on up the trail. Them of you that wants to can follow. Rest can go straight to —"

"Here's Odle now," Brinkman said coolly. "Let's see what he's got to say."

John Clancy swore under his breath. They should be out hunting for Seela and those damned outlaws instead of sitting around trying to figure where they went. Hell's bells! There was only one way they could have gone, and that was right on up the mountain. Maybe there weren't any tracks, but that didn't mean a damn thing. Being careful, they would have walked their horses off to the side in the leaves and pine needles that lay packed along the shoulder of the trail.

Clancy stirred impatiently and stared off into the shadowy depths of the mountainside into which Pete Odle had disappeared. He reckoned he was lucky they had Pete along. He had the reputation of being one of the best trappers in that part of the country. He was part Indian someone had said. Most likely it was true.

Clancy shifted his gaze to Harry Brinkman sitting quietly off to one side. Pete, being the best, worked for Brinkman — and that's what you'd expect. Brinkman had the best of everything. He owned one of the finest ranches; the miners he'd staked had all hit it big and paid off in gold even better than anyone had hoped for. Too, Brinkman drove the finest horses, had the latest thing in carriages, and dressed in the most expensive clothing. Harry could, and did, have everything he wanted — almost.

Clancy smiled secretly as that thought came to him. Brinkman had all those things, but he couldn't have the one thing he wanted most — Lorena. She was beyond his reach, and, knowing that, the fact gnawed at him like a festering sore. Maybe Brinkman had prospered the most after they had broken up their partnership, but Harry was still the loser, and that always made John Clancy feel good.

They had done real well when they were partners, Clancy thought, a bit of nostalgia and regret trickling through him. Leaving Tennessee and running into Brinkman one day in Missouri had been the best thing that had ever happened to him. Together they headed west, each with but one resolve in mind — to find gold, to strike it rich.

They'd had a hell of a good time pursuing the dream, drinking when they had felt like it, pairing off with saloon women when they'd had the notion and the money — working like field hands digging and slaving away shoulder to shoulder until they struck their bonanza.

He'd not soon forget that. As soon as they had their first big payoff, they went on a ten-day tear that folks in Solitude still talked about, spending money like it was going out of style, and everything was share and share alike.

Then Lorena had come into their lives.

Clancy couldn't recall exactly who had first seen her getting off the stagecoach from Lordsburg, but the moment he laid eyes on her — so trim in a pale blue suit that accented her curvaceous figure, her brown hair like a soft, misty halo about her head, and a perky little blue hat sitting slightly askew — he knew he was lost. At her side was a small child, her daughter he assumed.

Clancy remembered waiting, taut as a fiddle string, to see if a man followed her off the coach, and when none did, he joyously guessed she was a widow or, for some other reason, had no husband.

All the time he was feasting his eyes on Lorena and a turmoil within him was telling him that, at all costs, he must have her, Harry Brinkman was standing nearby and no doubt was entertaining the same thought. But it hadn't worked out the way Harry had hoped.

When they both pressed their suits for her hand, after she was settled and working at the Nugget, Lorena had eventually chosen him. That definitely established, Clancy, in a victorious and somewhat drunken celebration, and knowing how Brinkman felt about the lady, had warned his partner in no uncertain terms that their association was over unless he kept his distance insofar as Lorena was concerned, that she was his and his alone forevermore.

Clancy remembered how furious the usually calm and level-headed Brinkman had become at the ultimatum. One word had led to another and before the hour was over, he and Harry Brinkman had dissolved the partnership that had endured for so many years. Clancy had assured himself many times that it was something that had to be done. There simply was no room in his mind for a three-way friendship as the haunting question of why Lorena had chosen him over Brinkman plagued him constantly — and knowing little about women, he could never find the answer.

Once he had flatly asked Lorena for a reason. She had told him frankly that it was because he was a generous, happy man who had a smiling way about him, one who liked to dance, and, most important of all, she loved him.

That should have been answer enough, and he had thought so at that time. Brinkman was a sort of stern-faced man, serious to a fault. He cared little for dancing and socializing, but the fear that Lorena was regretting her choice was always with Clancy, particularly after his luck had turned sour and the gold in his mine had dwindled to little more than a daily pittance. All he and Lorena had then was the restaurant and the rooms above it. At Aaron

Plummer's suggestion, he had put the building and the business in Lorena's name, thus safeguarding it for as long as she wanted it.

Brinkman's luck had never failed him. He had gone into the cattle business and made a great deal of money supplying fresh beef to the mining camps and restaurants in the area, as well as to the Army. Too, he had controlling interests in just about every producing gold mine that amounted to anything — they having been acquired by clever maneuvering and a knack for backing the right people.

But he had Lorena, Clancy thought with satisfaction, and that was wealth enough for him. Brinkman had respected that fact and never, insofar as Clancy knew, made any attempt to even talk with Lorena, much less —

"Here's Odle now —"

Harry Brinkman's voice was, as always, even, quiet, and self-controlled and, for some reason since their parting, thoroughly irritated at John Clancy.

"Let's see what he's got to say."

"Don't look to me like he's come up with anything," Clancy said sourly. In the moonlight, he was a hunched, dejected figure in his saddle, one that portrayed his worry.

"Ain't done nothing but waste time setting here."

"The tracks show they doubled back," Odle said, addressing his remarks to Brinkman. "Crossed back over the trail. Now, way I see it, they rode into the creek so's to hide the tracks of their horses — leastwise all of them but one," he added, again holding his lantern low and studying the area along the stream. "Seems he kept up on the bank."

"That'd be Dagget trying to catch up with his partners," Speakman said.

There was a quick run of conversation among the riders after that comment. It was broken up by Clancy.

"All right," he said impatiently, "they didn't go on up the trail, they headed north with my girl. Come on, let's cut the jawing and get after them."

Brinkman nodded to Odle. "Best you lead off, Pete. If you figure it's best we all get off and walk so you won't lose the trail, just give the word. We can't —"

"Well, we ain't quitting until we find them," John Clancy declared. "And anybody that ain't of a mind to stick with me can turn back right now," he continued angrily as he swung his horse off the trail.

"Now, John, you know damn well there ain't none of us going to do that," Ed

Speakman said. "We're as anxious to catch up with that bunch and get your girl back as you are."

Clancy shook his head. "I ain't so sure of that. All the kowtowing that's been going on's got me to wondering."

Harry Brinkman shrugged and motioned for the riders to swing in behind Odle, already moving out. "Fall in behind Pete," he directed, his lips tight with anger. "We can leave it all up to him to keep us on the right track."

CHAPTER 10

Dagget froze. It was Jube Fowler's harsh voice.

"Me and Apache heard you a-skulking around out there in the brush for the last five minutes. Weren't fooling us none atall!"

Cole cursed himself silently. So intent had he been on Apache Reed that he had simply ignored Fowler and had carelessly assumed Jube would continue to sit by the fire.

"Step on out here where I can get a look at you, see just who the hell you are."

Dagget drew himself fully erect in the pale light and turned slowly. He was facing death, there was no doubt in his mind as to that. With all the outlaws had at stake, Jube would not hesitate to put a bullet into him. Arms still down and close to his sides, he calculated his chances for drawing his gun and firing before the outlaw could trigger his weapon. The odds that he could pull it off successfully were slim to none at all, he realized, but Cole Dagget, considering his immediate future on the earth under such circumstances, reckoned he had no choice but to try.

"Hey, Apache!" Jube called. "I got him!"

In the next fraction of time, Dagget threw himself to one side, drawing his gun while still in motion. Fowler's weapon blasted the quiet, the muzzle flash a bright orange in the half dark. Holding tight to his .45, Dagget rolled as the outlaw fired again, the bullet was close, dug into the weeds and litter only inches behind Cole.

"Over here, damn it!" Fowler yelled. "Apache — Cooter, get over here!"

Cole, on his knees behind a thick clump of oak brush, leveled his gun at the outlaw and pressed off a shot. Fowler yelled and staggered back. Raising his weapon, the outlaw drove a bullet into the clump of oak from which Dagget's shot had come.

But Dagget was no longer there. As powder smoke began to drift lazily above the brush and weeds, and the knowledge that both Reed and Cooter would be down on him shortly, backing Jube Fowler's play, Cole dropped to the ground and rolled again. One thing was certain in his mind, Jube had to be taken care of fast or he would be caught between the outlaw leader and his two partners.

Fowler fired again. Cole heard the bullet clip through the leaves of a wild raspberry bush. Bringing up his six-gun, he spun about and snapped a shot at the bright flash of the outlaw's weapon, vivid in the silvery darkness. Fowler yelled. A moment later, he staggered out from behind the tree that was affording him shelter. He paused, swayed drunkenly, and then fell heavily to the ground.

With smoke still curling about him, Cole reloaded his gun as he listened into the hush that had descended upon the area. Reed he thought, would be off somewhere to his left, Cooter to the right. But, of course, both having heard the gunshots, could have moved.

Which was exactly what he intended to do. Apache Reed and Cooter would come looking for him, and Dagget was determined not to make it easy for them. He figured it was better to be the hunter than the hunted. Bent low, Cole eased off through the brush and trees. When he'd seen Apache, the outlaw had been to the east of the camp and likely would still be in that neighborhood somewhere. Cooter, no doubt, was to the west and probably circling to the north. He'd think about the young outlaw later, after he had located and taken care of Reed — or, if things went wrong, Apache had gunned him down.

It was difficult to see for any distance. Trees grew thick in the swale, and brush and weeds pretty well covered the ground beneath them. Deep shadows were everywhere and as he worked his way slowly through the night, Cole was alert for any sound that would reveal the presence of Apache or Cooter.

Abruptly, a figure rose in the brush directly to his right. Cole recoiled and crouched. In the half-light he recognized Reed. The outlaw, startled, wheeled about.

"You!" he snarled. "Figured I killed you dead back there by the trail! I'll just —"

Dagget, cool as a morning's breeze, drove a bullet into the outlaw's chest. Reed rocked back from the impact of the .45's slug, muttered something unintelligible, and fell sideways.

Cole rode out a long minute while he, again, reloaded and listened for sounds of Cooter. Hearing nothing, and his gun still up and ready, he moved quietly up to where the outlaw lay sprawled across a low bush. As Dagget drew close, Reed's lifeless body suddenly slid off the clump of raspberry and fell to the leaf- and litter-covered ground.

Cole, stepping into a pool of darkness cast by a small cluster of pines, waited for Cooter. The young outlaw should be making some sort of move; the last gunshot would have given him an idea where his partners and the man at which they were shooting were.

Dagget continued to listen into the deep silence for indications of the outlaw's whereabouts. There was nothing, not even the clack of insects or the sleepy chittering of birds disturbed by the gunshots. Off to the west, coyotes were once again wailing in the moonlight, but they were miles away.

The quick hammer of horses racing into the night brought Cole up sharply. For a long moment, the beating sound of horses' hooves had no meaning, and then he realized Cooter was not somewhere nearby seeking to get a shot at him, but was making an escape — and that he had taken one of the other mounts for the girl to ride.

CHAPTER 11

"We could fix us a real fine life, just you and me," Cooter said coaxingly. "You'd be my missus — Mrs. Dave Cooter — now that sounds real good, don't it?"

Seela Clancy continued to sob, her shoulders shaking visibly as she struggled with fear and apprehension.

"Sure, I'm willing to get hitched," the outlaw continued, "if that's what you want. Don't see no need for it, however."

"I — I just — want to go home," Seela said brokenly. "Please — let me go — I'll find my way —"

"Sure have my misdoubts about that," Cooter replied, glancing off into the night. "There's a-plenty that could happen to you was you to head out through them hills in the dark. There's wolves and painters and wildcats, for one thing. Or maybe you'd run into a couple of hardcase miners who hadn't seen a woman for weeks. It'd pleasure them plenty to get their hands on a pretty young gal like you."

"I'll take my — chances —"

"Maybe you would, but I won't let you," Cooter said, his voice hardening. "Wouldn't be right. Besides, I took a fancy to you back there in that bank, and anybody that knows me will tell you that what I take a fancy to belongs to me — and mine to keep. You might just as well quit your bawling 'cause it ain't going to do you no good."

Dave Cooter paused and, moving slightly left, put his attention on the camp. Jube and Apache were still hunkered by the fire. As Cooter watched, Fowler poured a quantity of whiskey into the cup of coffee he was holding, took a long swallow, and settled back. Mixing liquor with coffee was a habit of Jube's, a combination that Dave had never been partial to; he liked his whiskey straight, just as he did his coffee.

The young outlaw grinned at the thought of the reactions he could expect from his two partners when he told them he aimed to make the girl, Seela — she had finally given him her name — his woman. He wasn't sure how they'd take it, but that didn't matter. As soon as Jube split up the money, something over ten thousand dollars apiece, he and Seela would pull out.

Ten thousand dollars — that was a hell of a lot of money! It was more than he had ever seen, much less ever dreamed of having. His folks had been Georgia sharecroppers, poor as Job's turkey, living from hand to mouth year after year. They, a family of nine, existed in a two-room shack, and there never was enough of anything to go around.

At the age of fifteen, Dave had taken his leave and shoved off into a world where survival was the most important of all factors. He had found life hard for a time while he drifted about fruitlessly seeking work of any kind and failing at everything from a lack of experience.

Eventually he turned to other means for staying alive. He stole a gun, a small, nickel-plated revolver from a drunken gambler he found sleeping in a shed at the rear of a saloon on the Texas-Mexico border. With it he pulled off several robberies, finding it not only amazingly easy, but well paying.

Subsequently, he met Jube Fowler and Apache Reed, and working with them he soon realized what it was like to be a big-time outlaw riding high with cash in his pockets and the heady thrill of knowing other men feared him and that the law was on his trail.

Jube was not only a good teacher, but a

good leader as well. He knew the country as well as he did the back of his hand, and he figured out the holdups and robberies they planned to such an exact point that not once were they ever caught. Apache Reed had once said that Jube —

"Why — why won't you let me go?" Seela's plaintive voice broke into his musing. "I won't ever cause you any trouble — I promise."

"Told you that ain't what I'm wanting," Cooter cut in angrily. "I'm wanting you for my woman — and that's just how it's going to be. Best you set your mind to that."

"But I — my folks'll pay —"

"They ain't got enough to buy you back from me, missy. Money don't mean nothing now. My share of the bank holdup's better'n ten thousand dollars, and I wasn't exactly busted flat when we pulled it off. I still had a couple of hundred left from the last job we pulled off.

"We'll be living on tall cotton with the money I'll have. Aim to do nothing but keep riding, moving, and seeing all the places I've heard folks talk about. Maybe even go back to St. Louis. We'll have us a fine time; figure on it!"

Seela Clancy shook her head despairingly. "It wouldn't be a fine life. The law will always be looking for you, and one day it'll find you and send you to prison for the things you've done."

"They ain't never going to catch me," Cooter said with a shrug. "Jube told me what it was like to be in the pen, and I sure don't aim to ever let them put me in one. He said he'd let hisself get blowed in two before he'd let the law dogs nail him again. Said he knew it would be either a hanging or back in the pen for him. Same goes for me."

"Maybe they wouldn't be so hard on you," Seela said, a note of hope in her voice. "You're young, not a lot older than me. You couldn't have done all the bad things that this Jube has done."

"Done my share," Dave said proudly. "Maybe I ain't been making my living with a gun as long as old Jube and Apache have — but I sure as hell ain't no greenhorn at it."

"My folks would help you, I promise," Seela insisted, as if not hearing Cooter's words. "We could leave right now — before the posse gets here —"

"Posse? What posse? Have you heard or seen any sign of one?"

"It's out there somewhere hunting us — and my pa won't quit till he finds me. If we leave now, we could —"

"I ain't about to leave — and neither are you! First time in my life I've got what I want — a pile of money and a young and pretty woman of my own. Sure not about to give any of it up."

"But I —"

Cooter raised his hand for silence and glanced toward the camp. Reed was not to be seen, but Jube Fowler had risen, crouched, then moved off slowly toward a stand of trees and brush. Drawing his gun, Cooter got to his feet.

"Stay put — right here," he said. "Something's wrong."

"It's probably my pa and the posse," the girl said, her spirits lifting. "I told you they'd be coming."

"Maybe," Cooter murmured, "but you best not bet on it . . . Now, I ain't going far so don't try running off."

Seela's shoulder tired. "No need to. My pa'll find me."

Cooter smiled tightly. "Now, I sure misdoubt that," he said, and hunched low, moved off into the brush and weeds, and began to circle toward the camp.

Maybe it was the posse, he thought, but it seemed hardly possible. How could they have found the camp so soon? Jube had led him and Apache across open, broken land well off the trail. It made no sense that the posse could have gotten on their trail so soon and tracked them to where they had camped. But something sure as hell was wrong; well away from the mound now, he paused. He could see no sign of Apache Reed and Jube looked to be closing in on somebody or something.

Fowler halted and squatted down in the brush. Moving quietly, Cooter worked in nearer. Suddenly Jube drew himself upright. He was poised there for a few brief seconds, a dark hunched shape silhouetted in the moonlight, and then two quick shots flatted through the night.

"Over here — dammit! Apache — Cooter — get over here!"

Another gunshot reawoke the dying echoes. Cooter saw Jube Fowler stagger and his intention to step in, to help Jube, wavered. Again Fowler triggered his weapon, and then once more. An answering shot came from the close-by brush. Cooter heard Jube yell and saw him stagger out into a small clearing near a thick tree. Fowler twisted half about and fell heavily. Dave Cooter swore deeply; Fowler was dead, there was little doubt of that. Dave waited, motionless. Another gunshot broke the hush shortly, coming from somewhere off to the left of where he had seen Jube fall.

That could be a bullet cutting down Apache Reed, Cooter reckoned. He'd not been seen or heard from despite Fowler's yell for help. It had to be the posse closing in although it was still a mystery to Dave how they could have located the camp so readily and so soon. But that meant nothing to him now.

Wheeling, and staying low, he doubled back to where Jube and Apache had tethered their horses. The money would be in the saddlebags on Fowler's horse; Cooter had seen Jube fill them at the bank and then hang the leather pouches across his saddle. Freeing the lines which Jube had wound into a clump of sledge growing along the creek, he hurried back to where he had left the girl, collecting his own mount on the way.

"Get up!" he ordered, halting in front of Seela. "You're going to ride Jube's horse."

The girl stared up at him. "Why — what's happened? Is it the posse?"

Cooter reached down, seized her by the arm, and jerked her to her feet. "No, it ain't no posse!" he answered, and shoved her toward the bay Fowler had been riding. "Climb up into the saddle or I'll knock you cold and put you there myself!"

Seela moved to the side of the bay. Reaching for the saddlehorn, she made an attempt to mount but failed. Cursing, Cooter placed both hands on her buttocks and boosted her into the saddle. At once he turned to his own horse and, taking up the reins of Fowler's bay, rode out of the clearing behind the weedy mound into the deeper shadows along the water's edge.

"You can ride like that if you behave," Cooter said, pulling the saddlebags from Jube's saddle and hanging them across his own hull as they crossed the creek. "Howsomever, if you make a try to get away, I'll real quick tie your hands to that saddle's gullet. You hear?"

Seela, casting a despairing glance over her shoulder in the direction of the camp, clutched at the horn and nodded.

"Just you remember that," Cooter continued, spurring his horse into a gallop and forcing Seela's mount to follow at a like pace.

He'd be a fool to put too much trust in the girl, not until he had her well away from any possibility of the posse finding them. By then, she would have decided there was no hope of her pa and the others helping her, and there was nothing to do but comply with his orders.

A break in the brush along the foot of the moonlit slope just ahead indicated a trail of some sort — a path deer and other animals used, he guessed, and veered his horse toward it. As soon as they were well up the mountainside and there was no sign of the posse in pursuit, he'd stop and tie the girl's hands to the fork of her saddle anyway. The way matters were shaping up, he couldn't afford to gamble on her causing trouble.

Dave felt a surge of elation race through him. The posse had no idea where he was, he had all of the money stolen from the bank, all thirty thousand dollars of it — and he had the girl. Jube Fowler was dead and, most likely, Apache Reed was in the hands of the posse with nothing ahead for him but a hangman's rope — if he, too, wasn't already dead.

Cooter felt like yelling for joy. For him, the future now held something else — the girl who had caught his fancy, and money enough to last for a long time. What could be better?

CHAPTER 12

Leaving the shadows in which he was standing, Cole circled quickly back to the camp. The fire was almost out, but it took only a glance beyond it to see the dark outline of only one horse by the creek where earlier there had been two. What he had assumed was true; Cooter, to take the load off his horse, encumbered and slowed by carrying double, had appropriated one of the other animals, either Reed's or Jube Fowler's.

Dagget wheeled and started for his horse, the intention to go after the outlaw and the girl foremost in his mind. He halted, indecision filling him. Following them would be difficult. He had no idea of the direction they had taken after crossing the creek; they could have gone left, right, or up the slope. It would be a matter of tracking, and that, too, on the shadowy mountainside with its floor covered with pine needles, leaves, and other forest debris would be next to impossible.

He glanced to the east. First light was still hours away, but there was not much use trying to locate Cooter's trail until then. The white grub sack that Fowler had spoken of lay on the ground near the fire. Crossing to it, Dagget picked it up, untied the string that closed its neck, and thrust his hand inside. A tight grin cracked his lips as his fingers came in contact with packets of currency, several loose bills, and coins.

On impulse, he turned the grub sack upside down and dumped its contents on the ground. The coins glittered softly in the light of the low fire, but he gave them little notice, his attention, instead, being on the currency.

Thirty thousand dollars, someone had said. A man could build himself not only a fine ranch but create an empire for himself with that much money! Dagget grinned again. What the hell was he thinking of? The money in no way could ever be his. He'd like to look forward to sleeping nights and not spending the rest of his days looking over his shoulder because he had committed a robbery by taking the bank's money for his own. Laying the grub sack aside, he began to pick up the loose bills and count out the eight hundred dollars that was rightfully his. When he had the correct amount, Cole folded the bills, drew off his money belt, and stored them inside where they would be safe. That done, he restored the remainder of the money to the grub sack.

The thought came to him then that he was free to hurry on now, get to the ranch in Mangas Springs, and close the deal for the horses he so badly needed — assuming no other buyer had come along during the time he'd lost chasing Jube Fowler and his partners and recovering his money. That had cost him at least a day.

The bank's money — what should he do about it? The posse would be along eventually, he reckoned; he could leave the flour sack containing the currency and coins in plain view with the bodies of Fowler and Apache Reed. In that way, the cash could be recovered and returned to the bank.

Dagget stared into the fire and gave that consideration. Quiet had returned to the clearing and nearby brush and trees. The insects had resumed their clacking and birds had settled down. An owl hooted forlornly among the pines off to the east, and well into the opposite direction, the coyotes were continuing their discordant chorus.

The girl — Seela. In his joy at recovering the eight hundred dollars and reviving the prospect of getting to Mangas Springs in time, he had forgotten all about her.

That threw a different light on things — was a mule with longer ears, as an old bronc buster with whom he was acquainted was wont to say. It meant more delay, for to move out at first light and start a search for her and the outlaw would consume another day at least, possibly longer. He could expect Cooter to avoid leaving any hoofprints of their horses and, too, they would be traveling fast since Seela now had a mount of her own.

Cole shifted his glance into the direction of the Escondido Trail, hopeful of seeing some indication of the posse. There was no sign of the riders either on the slopes or out on the flats. It was becoming apparent to Dagget that the party had missed his sign at the fork and had continued along the Socorro road, or coming up the Escondido had overridden the point by the creek where he and the outlaws had turned north.

Dagget swore raggedly. He had important business of his own to attend to and simply couldn't afford to go chasing off into the hills after Seela and Cooter. Likely, it would prove to be fruitless, anyway.

A guilt reaction washed through Cole Dagget. "Hell no!" he muttered aloud, he couldn't ignore the plight of the Clancy girl. It was time, under the circumstances, that he stopped thinking only of himself and faced up to what was the decent thing for a man to do — and that was to do all he could for Seela. He had been so intent on his own interests that he was overlooking an obvious duty.

Perhaps it would all turn out right anyway. If he could be lucky enough to track down Cooter and the girl right away, or if the posse showed up, he could then strike out immediately for Mangas Springs, and if he were doubly lucky, the horses he was hoping to buy would still be available. Meantime, he'd do what he could to put the posse on the right track.

Throwing what was left of the wood supply Apache Reed had provided onto the fire, Dagget hurried to where Jube Fowler lay. Taking the body by the heels, he dragged it back to the camp and laid it out near the fire. Going then to Apache Reed, he followed a like procedure, placing the outlaw's limp body alongside that of his partner Jube.

A big fire would be the best means for attracting the posse, he reasoned. It should be arranged in such a fashion that it would burn for a considerable time. At once, Cole began to fan out from the camp and bring in all the wood that he could find which he laid at the end of the fire in a lengthy, extending line. By so doing, he would create a chain reaction of flames that would continue to blaze up for what he hoped would be hours. If any member of the posse were anywhere on the trail or the side of the mountain, he would have no trouble seeing the fire or its glow and hopefully quickly investigate.

Tracks would make it clear which direction the outlaw and his hostage had taken. The bodies of Fowler and Reed would tell them that Cooter, alone, had the girl, and if they read the prints correctly, they would see that he was on the outlaw's trail ahead of them. With all that information before them, the posse should have no trouble following.

Cole glanced about and saw that the fire was doing well. Sweating from his labors, despite the coolness of the night, he pivoted on a heel and started for his horse. Abruptly he halted. The bank's money — would it be safe to leave it there beside the bodies of the two outlaws?

Probably not, Cole decided. Not all men were honest, and thirty thousand dollars was a prize that would tempt even the most law-abiding man who might come along while searching for the girl and her captor. Should the entire posse arrive on the scene together, there was little doubt the money would be safe and eventually returned to the bank, but there was no real assurance that such would be the case.

With the fire crackling noisily and sending up a bright yellowish flare into the night, Cole took up the grub sack containing the money and carried it to where he had left his horse. Unbuckling one of his saddlebag pockets, he placed the sack inside, refastened the straps, and swung up onto the buckskin.

Cutting about, he threw his glance to the east. It was still some time until the first light when he had planned to begin his search for Seela Clancy and Cooter. But he could see no reason for hanging around the camp any longer; he had done all he could, and he just might get lucky right off the bat and find the tracks of —

The sound of voices reached Dagget. The posse! That thought came first to Cole's mind, and then he realized he had heard no horses and there seemed to be only two people. Still in the shadows several yards from the camp where he had left the buckskin, Dagget waited. If it was the posse, or just a couple of members sent to investigate the fire, his problem would be solved. He could make his explanation what had happened, turn the money over to them, and be on his way.

But it was not to be, Dagget realized with a heavy sigh. Nothing seemed to go right for him. The voices had come from two men, drifters or down-on-their-luck miners, judging from their appearance. They approached the fire cautiously, and seeing the bodies of Jube Fowler and Apache Reed, drew back suddenly.

"Hell, we sure ain't got no business being here!" the taller of the pair said. "There's a killer around somewheres."

"Looks like he's done gone now," the other replied with a shrug. "Murdered these two fellows then took off. Let's see if there's anything in their pockets."

"What if somebody comes along? They'll figure for sure we done the killings."

"Now, who the hell's going to be coming along here this time of the night!" the tall man's companion, a heavyset, bearded individual in worn overalls, a faded linsey-woolsey shirt and a slouch cap, said dismounting. "We're a far piece from the trail, and there ain't nothing around here but red wolves, coyotes, and us. I'm going to have myself a look."

"Don't see no use of that. If they've already been robbed, there won't be nothing —"

"Maybe it weren't no robbery, just a killing. Anyway, there could be something they overlooked. Needing cash like I do, I sure don't aim to pass up anything."

"Well, maybe you're right," the tall one said, coming down off his horse. He was dressed similarly except that on his head he wore an old army campaign hat. Moving to where his friend was kneeling beside the body of Jube Fowler, he squatted beside that of Apache Reed. After a few minutes, he got to his feet.

"Ain't nothing on this one but a beat-up old jackknife and a couple of poker chips."

"Ain't much more'n that on this one — about a dollar in loose change . . . Why you reckon they made such a big fire?" he added, attention shifting to the flames. "Sure kind of funny the way it's all strung out like it is."

"Like it was a signal of some kind —"

"Expect that's just what it is."

The tall one glanced about worriedly. "Will, we best get the hell out of here. I got me a feeling that something bad's going to happen."

"Seems to me it already has," Will said

dryly, crossing to his horse. "That there big fire is fixed so's it'll burn for a long time, and that sure means something!"

"Sure does," the tall man said, hurrying to his mount and climbing quickly into the saddle, "and whatever it is, I ain't anxious to find out —"

The drifter's voice died off into silence as Cole rode out of the brush into the circle of light thrown by the fire. Both men stiffened.

"Now, mister, we didn't have no hand in these killings!" Will said hastily. "We was just riding by, seen the fire, and —"

"I'm not saying you did," Dagget cut in.

The squat man's shoulders relaxed slightly, but his features remained stiff and drawn with worry. "Well, if it was you, me and Bert ain't seen nothing. No sir, nothing!"

Dagget shook his head. "You headed south for the trail?"

"Sure. Aiming to go to Silvertown."

"You can do me a favor. There's a posse headed this way. Like for you to tell them where this camp is and that you saw me."

"Seen you? If it's a bunch of lawmen a-looking for you, why —"

"Not after me. After those two I had to shoot, and another one that stole a girl. Tell them when they get here to keep going west

— up that slope — best they look for tracks."

"You saying you killed them two laying there on the ground?" the one named Bert asked.

Dagget shrugged. The knowledge that he had killed two men had been lying in the back of his mind from the moment the incident was over, hanging there like a dark, accusing shadow. Now to hear it voiced in words by another man brought it more forcibly to his conscience. He had never killed before and even though this had been a matter of shoot or get shot, he was finding little solace in that fact.

"Had no choice —"

"I reckon it's your business," Will said.

Cole nodded. "I'll be obliged to you if you'll look up the posse and tell them what I said."

"I reckon we can. Could sort of turn out to be a mite out of our way —"

Dagget reached into his pocket and produced two silver dollars and flipped one to each of the men. "Maybe this'll pay you for your trouble."

"Yes sir, it sure will!" Bert said with a wide grin. "Yes sir! Come on, Will, let's get moving."

Will swung in behind his partner. "And

we're obliged to you, mister. Can bank on us doing just what you asked — even if we have to hunt up that posse . . . Adios."

CHAPTER 13

Dagget watched the drifters ride off into the moonlight-dappled brush and trees below the camp. Maybe they would encounter the posse and perhaps they would not — he gave no credence to their promise to seek out the party and relay his message. But there was a chance they would meet and if this happened, the posse would find itself on the right track.

He threw a final glance at the fire, saw that the flames were good for another hour or so, and then swinging about, struck for the slope looming up darkly some hundred yards or so away. The fact that Cooter and Seela Clancy had so quickly managed to disappear on the mountain's side would indicate the presence of a trail. If he could locate it without any great delay, he just might catch up with the outlaw and free the girl who, by that time, was probably in very poor condition.

As he came to the creek, the lone horse —
Fowler's or Apache Reed's, he didn't know
which — nickered anxiously. The animal
shouldn't be left tied as it was, it needed to
be free to graze. Cutting over to where the
horse, a dark shape in the pale night, was
standing, Dagget dismounted and, pulling
the reins loose, secured them to the saddle
horn so they could not become entangled
in the brush. Returning to the buckskin, he
swung aboard and, fording the creek, continued on across the open ground for the
slope.

Halting at its base, Cole studied the
mountainside. It was thickly forested and
covered by brush. At first glance, there appeared to be no break, no trail anywhere.
Again dismounting, he began to cover the
base of the slope step by step. It was costing
time, Dagget was aware of that fact, but he
had to be dead-sure; every minute Seela
Clancy was in the hands of Dave Cooter
would be like a day in hell to her — not to
mention the cost of any delay to him. He
had to be right; to get off on the wrong trail,
or in the wrong direction, would be the
worst possible thing he could do.

Moving slowly, eyes on the soft ground all
around him, Cole examined the foot of the
slope. A grin of satisfaction cracked his lips.

In the weak silver light, an opening between two fair-sized boulders caught his eye. Kneeling, he scrutinized the ground closely. He smiled again. Imprinted clearly in the dark soil were the hoofprints of two horses and those of a deer that had earlier preceded them up the trail.

Going back into the saddle, Dagget started up the path. It was narrow with rocks and brush bordering closely on either side, and as the buckskin climbed steadily, the trail grew even more confined and steeper. Cooter and the girl could not have cut away anywhere along the path so far, Cole reasoned when he halted to breathe the buckskin an hour or so later. They would still be somewhere ahead.

He listened often for any sounds of their passage but heard nothing. There should have been the rattle of displaced gravel, it would seem, or an occasional crackling of brush, but since there had been neither, he just assumed the pair were too far ahead and above him.

He reckoned he was hoping for too much in expecting to hear their movements. Cooter had rushed off with the girl shortly after the shooting had taken place, electing to ignore Jube Fowler's call for help. He had lost no time in loading Seela onto a horse belonging to one of his partners, likely Jube's.

Dagget smiled as a thought came to him. Most likely Cooter had chosen Fowler's mount for the girl in the belief the money stolen from the bank was on it. Taking the girl and moving off behind the high weed and rock-covered mound where his partners could not see him, he would not have known that Fowler had removed the money from the saddlebags he had used at the bank and stashed it away in a grub sack for safe keeping.

Cooter was in for a big surprise when he discovered there was no cash — something Cole was certain the outlaw had figured on. Dave Cooter wouldn't have passed up the chance to take both the money and the girl when the opportunity was handed to him.

The trail wound on up the side of the mountain, at times climbing steeply, on other occasions slicing laterally across the slope. Coyotes continuously barked from the higher ledges and swales, and now and then a wolf voiced his eerie complaint.

The night wore off slowly as the buckskin continued to follow the path. A slight wind came up, laying a chill in the air, causing Dagget to pull the wool poncho from its place behind the saddle's cantle, drop it over his head, and let it settle about his shoulders.

It was necessary to halt now and then and allow the buckskin to rest. The trail had become steeper as they neared its summit, and there were places where loose shale or a sharp slant in the path made it wise to leave the saddle and lead the horse until they were once again on secure footing. Such conditions would have slowed Cooter and the girl, too, Dagget reasoned, so he would at least be holding his own insofar as time was concerned.

Daylight came slowly, lighting first the towering peaks and then gradually working down the slopes to the valleys and plains. At the spread of light on an open strip of the trail, Cole pulled to a halt, dismounted, and made a quick examination of the path.

A curse exploded from his lips. The deer tracks were there and easily read, but no longer were there any hoofprints. Dagget drew himself erect and looked off down the slope. Somewhere along the way, in the half dark, he had overridden the point where the outlaw and the girl had turned off. He couldn't recall any place along the trail where that could have been possible as there was no break in the closely crowding brush and rocks, but it had to be. He had simply, perhaps dozing at the time, missed it.

Turning the buckskin around, Dagget started back down the narrow path, eyes fixed on the uneven ground before him. All around he could hear the birds and insects coming to life as the warming rays of the sun probed into the trees and bushes and stirred them into activity. The coyotes and wolves had ceased their serenading with the arrival of day and no doubt had turned now to foraging for food, while high overhead in the cloudless sky a flock of ducks were hurrying across the blue background for some lake or stream in the area.

Dagget retraced the hoofprints of the buckskin for a long quarter mile. Worn and breathing hard from the unaccustomed walking, he was about to climb back into the saddle when a confusion of tracks near a large rock drew his attention. Turning away from his horse, he hurried to the prints and, hunched low, began to puzzle them out.

It took only moments. Just beyond the boulder was a trail angling off to the north. Cole, bent low and again leading his horse, moved onto it. He stopped abruptly. Directly ahead were the hoofprints of two horses — doubtlessly made by those being ridden by Seela and the outlaw, but he had to be sure. Bending lower, he touched the edge of the nearest print. It crumbled under the slight pressure of his finger.

Dagget straightened up. There could be no question. Two riders had passed that way only an hour or so earlier. And, all things considered, it could only have been Dave Cooter and Seela Clancy.

Weariness now dragging at him, Dagget climbed back into the saddle and continued along the trail. It ran fairly level across the side of the slope for a short distance and then topping out a ridge, dropped gently off into a wide, rocky canyon. The buckskin gelding found the going easy as the trail was downgrade, and while not smooth, presented no difficult footing. In a very short time, they reached the floor of the wide cut and were following it as it continued northward.

A few minutes later, Cole caught the smell of woodsmoke in the cool air and, slowing his horse, searched ahead for signs of someone. That effort failed, but a half mile farther on he came to a small, crude sign bearing the faded lettering GOLD CREEK CAMP and pointing on up the canyon that was gradually widening into a valley.

Dagget gave that consideration and then, after a brief time, moved on. The fear that

128

he had followed two miners off the trail, that Cooter and the girl had turned from the steep, rugged path even earlier, began to haunt him. But he had no choice other than to continue and find out for certain if he had made a mistake. If so, he could forget —

Rounding a clump of wild cherry, Dagget came to a halt. A shack with two horses alongside stood in the swale between the close by hills to the left. On ahead were several other shacks — the source of the smoke he had smelled.

But he was not interested in them. The two horses had to be those of Cooter and the girl. He hadn't paid too much attention to the outlaw horses back in the camp, but he did recall that Cooter had been riding a pinto and the ones picketed by the stream were dark — possibly a bay and a sorrel.

Staying in the trees and thick brush, he skirted the open ground and rode in as near as he deemed prudent to the cabin. Halting, he tied the worn buckskin to the stump of a lightning-blackened pine and, working himself in to the shack, peered through the single window facing him on the near side of the aged structure.

Something akin to elation rolled through him. He had been right. Cowering in a back corner of the dusty, one-room shack was

Seela Clancy. Disheveled in her ragged and dirty clothing, she was wearing a wool bush jacket that Cooter had apparently given her. Her dust-streaked face showed the weariness that gripped her, and her face bore a dark bruise on one side where the outlaw had evidently struck her. There could be more evidence of Cooter's brutality not visible to him, Cole realized, but for the moment that did not matter; the important thing was that he had caught up with them.

Dropping his hand to the gun on his hip, Dagget started to draw the weapon and cross to the door. The hard, round feel of a rifle barrel pressing into his spine brought him up short. A moment later, the harsh voice of a man holding the weapon, reached him.

"Just forget about that there iron, cowboy — unless you want me to blow you into hades! . . . Get that pistol of his, Zeke, then we'll see just what this here is all about."

CHAPTER 14

Dagget felt the weight on his hip lessen as the .45 was lifted from the holster. A hand dropped heavily on his shoulder and jerked him around.

"I don't know what you're up to, friend, but I reckon it ain't to no good . . . Knock on the door, Zeke. Let's talk to them folks we seen going in there."

Zeke, a thick, bandy-legged man in bib overalls, a coarse shirt, and heavy boots, shuffled over to the door and rapped loudly. There was no immediate response. The miner knocked again, more insistently.

"What do you want?" Dave Cooter's voice contained a note of anger, as well as caution.

"Name's Williams," the man with the rifle replied. "Me and my partner was out back when you and your woman rode in a bit ago. Then we seen this here jasper a-skulking around and looking through the window.

131

Figured you'd want to know what the hell he's up to."

"That man in there's an outlaw!" Dagget said, hanging tight to the fury and frustration that gripped him. "He robbed the bank in Solitude — and kidnapped that girl he's got with him."

"Do tell!" Williams said mildly. "Well, we'll just see what he's got to say about that."

"He sure don't look like no outlaw," Zeke commented. "Me and Josh just figured they was a couple looking for a place to sleep. Gal don't look like she's just been stole either."

"What the hell should she look like —" Dagget began, and then hushed as the door opened.

As its rusting, squeaking hinges grated noisily, Dave Cooter started to step out into the open, but Williams, prodding Cole with the rifle barrel, forced him past the outlaw and into the cabin. Zeke, following, kicked the sagging old panel closed.

"You know this bird, lady?" Williams asked.

Seela Clancy was still crouched in the back corner of the dusty, stale-smelling room. She didn't look up as the men halted before her.

"Sure she knows him!" Cooter said loudly. "He's been ragging her to marry-up with him for most a year. Picked me instead."

"That right?" Williams pressed. Wearing an old slouch hat, denim pants, heavy boots, a plaid shirt and a red-and-blue checked mackinaw, it was evident, too, that he was a miner.

Seela hesitated, raised her tear-streaked face, and nodded weakly.

"You all have got her half-scared to death," Cooter said. "You a-busting in here like you did, and him a chasing us halfway across the territory. Hell, we ain't had a bit of rest."

Williams lowered his rifle. "Then what this here fellow says is a lie — that you robbed a bank and stole the girl —"

"You're damn right he's lying!" Cooter declared. "It's just like I'm telling you. He was after marrying-up with her, but she didn't want no part of him. We figured we'd fix him up for good by running off and getting hitched, but soon as he found out what we'd done, he took out after us. Been dogging our tracks ever since. I reckon what he wants to do is try talking her out of marrying-up with me, and if she won't listen, then make a widow out of her."

"You married now?"

"Well, not exactly. Ain't come to no town

where there's a preacher. Been hoping to find one."

"He's a liar," Dagget said flatly. "His name's Dave Cooter and he and his two partners robbed the bank in Solitude, just like I said. Killed a man there and rode off with the girl."

"Solitude?" Zeke murmured. "Ain't that a place down near Silvertown?"

Cole nodded. "The girl there is Seela Clancy. She's the daughter of —"

"You a lawman?" Williams asked.

"No, happened to be in the bank when they held it up. They got some money of mine and I —"

"He's the one what's doing the lying," Cooter broke in, his voice firm and convincing. "Weren't no bank robbery that I know of and, if there was, he probably done it. And I sure didn't steal this gal — Seela her name is. She's been mine all along."

"What about the two men he said was your partners?"

"Don't know nothing about them. We did just sort of run into a couple of fellows on the trail. Made camp together one night then this here jasper showed up and started giving us a pack of trouble. When they seen what it was all about, they grabbed him and told us to skedaddle. Said they'd hold him

134

till daylight so's we could get a good start.

"We done just that — rode all night. Was aiming to put up in this old shack and get a little sleep. My woman is sure tired out from running from him."

"What about it?" Josh Williams demanded, again prodding Dagget with his rifle. "What've you got to say to all that?"

"One thing — it's a lie, every bit of it," Cole answered in a low, savage tone. "You ought to be able to see that."

"I'm betting he killed them two nice fellows that tried to help us," Cooter said. "He's a bad one. Somehow he got the drop on them and sent them both to glory. And if he did, I sure do hate it. They was only trying to help me and the — and Seela."

Josh Williams shook his head. "I sure don't know just who's telling the truth here, but I'm sort of leaning toward the young fellow and the girl. Makes more sense."

"Yeah," Zeke said, "if it was like the cowboy says, there'd be a posse on their trail."

"There is," Cole said, hope rising within him. "I just left signs along the trail for them to follow. Look for them to be showing up pretty soon."

Williams shrugged. "Seems to me if there

was a posse, they'd have showed up before now."

"Well, if there is," Cooter said, "it's him they're looking for, not me. This jasper's saying all them things about me and my woman just to save his own hide. He knows he'd done wrong — not just trying to stop me from getting hitched with my girl, but like as not he's wanted for murdering a few other men besides them two that tried to help us."

"Like I said, it makes sense to me," Williams commented, and prodded Cole again. "Ain't you got a name?"

"Nobody asked," Cole snapped, "but I'm Cole Dagget. Deal in horses — and if you jab me with that damned gun once more, I'm going to take it away from you and bend it over your head!"

"You've got a hard mouth!" Williams said.

"And a mighty slick tongue," Cooter added. "Best you watch out for him . . . There a chance I could talk you two gents into tying him up and holding onto him for a spell so's the little lady and me could get on our way? Ain't neither one of us feeling like sleeping now."

Williams and Zeke exchanged glances. "Don't see why not," the latter said. "We can trot him over to our cabin and keep him there for a spell."

"Till tomorrow morning would be fine," Cooter said. "We sure would be mightily obliged."

Dagget shook his head angrily. "If you listen to him, you'll be making a big mistake!" he said in a hard voice. "What I've told you is true. Cooter there is an outlaw — and he stole that girl. Maybe I did kill his partners, but it was either them or me —"

"See, what'd I tell you?" Cooter said, grinning. "He murdered them two nice fellows just like I figured he'd do!"

Zeke nodded. "You was sure right there —"

"I expect it'd be a right good idea for you to hang onto him, and turn him over to the nearest sheriff," Cooter continued, moving toward the girl. "Like as not, there's a big reward for a killer like him."

Williams's bewhiskered features brightened. "Now that's a right smart idea. I'll just bet there is."

"Sure would pay to find out. Just could turn out that you'd end up with a pile of cash catching yourself a curly wolf like him . . . Now, if we're done palavering, I think me and my woman'll ride on while you and your partner there hog-tie and hang onto Dagget."

"Just you do what you please. Up to you."

"Could be we can find us that preacher we've been looking for and get this marrying-up business done with."

Dagget, taut with anger, shook off Zeke's broad hand that seized his arm. "You'll be letting an outlaw — a killer, go free," he said, voice trembling with anger. "And that girl — can't you see she's only a kid — a youngster, and that he's got her so scared of him that she can't talk?"

"All I can see is that you're butting in on something that you ain't got no business doing," Williams said. "Open the door, Zeke. Let's march him over to our place and bed him down real comfortable . . . Now move, Dagget — or whatever you call yourself," he added to Cole, gesturing with his rifle.

For a moment, Cole was too furious to stir. That Josh Williams and Zeke couldn't see through the outlaw's farfetched tale was hard to believe, but they hadn't, and he, for the moment, had no choice other than to turn about and step through the open doorway into the yard. One thing, he thought with a hard grin, he had evidently convinced Josh Williams to forgo using his rifle as a prod.

"Get his horse," Williams said to Zeke. "It's that buckskin over there in the brush."

"I know," Zeke said. "Was right here when he rode up on him."

Under the threat of the rifle's muzzle, Dagget waited while Zeke trotted over to where he had left his horse. His anger had leveled off into a sullen rage within him, and frustration was having its strong way with him. It was useless to try and talk to Williams and his partner. They took no stock in anything he told them but swallowed Dave Cooter's lies without the slightest hesitation.

And Seela Clancy had been of no help. It was clear she was too frightened of Cooter to say anything, and could only nod or shake her head when he demanded verification of something he had said. But the matter was far from over. The two miners figured to take him to their cabin — keeping him there would be a horse of a different color — he'd see to that.

Meanwhile, Cooter was being smart and, taking Seela, was moving on. They'd have a head start on him again, but it had been that way before. He'd keep after them until he caught up once more and next time he would see to it that Seela Clancy gained her freedom from the outlaw even if he had to kill again.

CHAPTER 15

Dave Cooter closed the door behind the two miners and Dagget. He wheeled swiftly to Seela.

"Get up! We're leaving here — fast. And cut out that damned bawling unless you want me to slap your jaws good again!"

Reaching down, he took the unresponsive girl by the hand and jerked her upright. "Damn it!" he snarled in a low, angry voice. "You best start behaving and doing what I tell you to do or you're going to be mighty sorry!"

"I — I don't —" Seela began haltingly.

"I don't give a hoot 'bout what you don't want! You're doing just what I tell you to, hear?"

Seela, head down, nodded sullenly. Cooter turned and crossed to the door. Opening it a crack, he looked out. The two miners and Cole Dagget were just disappearing behind a clump of juniper. In another moment, they would be out of sight. Pivoting, he faced the girl.

"Come on, we're moving out," he said, pushing Seela toward the door.

"I'm so tired," she murmured, holding back. "Can't we rest here for a little while?"

Cooter grinned. "You're thinking maybe Dagget can get hisself loose and come here to help you again — that it?"

The girl shrugged indifferently. "I'm so tired, I don't care much about anything. I — I want to sleep."

"Or maybe you figure a posse'll catch up?"

She raised her head, looked at him. The dirt and dust streaks still marked her child-like face, and she had made no effort to fix her hair. It still drooped loosely about her head.

"Posse? I thought you said there wasn't —"

"There ain't none so forget it. And you can sleep while you're riding," Cooter snapped. "Hell, I'm beat, too, but I ain't quitting. No sir! Not until we're a far piece from here, living high on the hog with all this money," he added, patting the saddle-bags he'd taken off Fowler's horse and that now hung across his shoulder.

Delaying no longer, he seized the girl by the arm and drew her with him to the door.

Again, cracking it narrowly, he glanced out.

"They're gone," he said, pulling the weathered, splintered old panel back. "Now's the time for us to move."

Grasping Seela firmly by her upper arm, he stepped out into the open and hurriedly crossed the front of the cabin. Rounding its corner, he crossed to where he had tied the horses. Boosting Seela up into the saddle of Jube's bay, he got her small feet into the loops in the leather above the stirrups, and set her hands on the horn. She made no effort to either aid or resist, but sat there woodenly and allowed him to do with her as he wished.

"You want me to tie you to that saddle so's you won't fall off?" he asked, stepping back.

Seela gave him no answer. Swearing, Cooter stepped to his horse, dug into the saddlebags, and produced a short length of rawhide cord.

"Expect I best cinch you down," he said, wrapping the leather about her wrists and securing the loose ends to the gullet. "If this don't keep you on your horse, I can tie your feet to the cinch, too."

"Do we have to go far?" she asked in a despondent, dragging voice.

"I reckon that all depends," Cooter replied. "If there's a posse chasing us, we'll just keep on going."

"Then there is a posse!"

"Ain't saying there is and I ain't saying there ain't. But it don't mean nothing. They'll never catch up with us no more'n that Dagget'll ever see us again."

Seela shook her head slightly and allowed her body to slump in a sign of hopeless resignation. The outlaw turned to his pinto and swung up onto the horse.

"Maybe we won't have to keep riding much longer," he said in an attempt at gentleness, taking up the reins to her horse in his right hand as he gathered up the pinto's lines in his left. "There's a lot of old cabins like the one we was just in scattered through these hills. Soon as I'm sure there ain't nobody dogging us, I'll find one and we can bed down for a couple of days. That suit you?"

Seela did not reply. A hard grin pulled at Dave Cooter's lips. "You don't act real pleased at the idea! Well, you best start liking it because me and you'll be bedding down together a lot from now on."

The outlaw waited for some reaction or comment from the girl and, when none came, looked ahead. They had crossed the last strip of open ground and a fairly good trail leading up the mountain was just ahead. It would lead to somewhere, Cooter reasoned as he turned on to it. Twisting about, he glanced past Seela, hunched and already dozing in her saddle. There was no sign of the miners, Williams and his partner, Zeke, and, of course, none of Cole Dagget. There was only a spiral of thin blue smoke twisting up from one of the cabins.

Around midday they topped out the mountain and began a slow descent of the opposite side. The day had turned cool and cloudy and, pulling to a slight mound off to one side, he turned his attention back into the direction of the camp and valley searching for any sign of pursuit.

He could see no indication of any, and now was well satisfied that if a party of armed men from Solitude was hunting for him, they had evidently headed off in the wrong direction — probably at that fork in the main road where the right hand led on to Socorro and points east. He reckoned he could ignore that troublesome feeling, so recently alive in his mind, that there was a posse closing in on him, and start taking it easier. Dagget was taken care of and there really was no need to keep riding.

He began to look for a place where he and the girl could hole up and rest for a bit. He was hungry and he suspected the girl was in need of food also. He had a few strips of jerky, some dry biscuits, and a sack of coffee beans in his saddlebags, and with that they'd make do. Later they'd ride on and find some town where he could lay in a supply of grub.

Maybe it wouldn't be necessary to buy up any trail grub. After they'd caught up on their rest and sleep, why shouldn't they move on to the nearest town? With all the money he had now they could eat in restaurants, sleep in hotels, and live like quality folks. They could buy themselves some new clothes, trade the saddle Seela was using for one that fit her, and when they got tired of where they were, ride on.

It would be a great way to live, a good life, the kind he'd always dreamed of, and with a young girl like Seela at his side, it would be doubly enjoyable. She would be all for it, too, as soon as she realized what plans he had made and what it would mean for her. No more living in a one-horse town like Solitude, but being on the move, seeing all the places she'd likely dreamed of — and when the time came to stop drifting and settle down, pick one of the big towns like Denver or San Antonio, or maybe Dodge City.

Cooter felt a raindrop dash against his face. He glanced up. The sky had gathered an overcast. As the shower increased in intensity, Dave began to look about, to search the slopes and open areas for a shelter of some sort. It would be smart to get out of the wet until it cleared up. He caught sight of a cabin, actually a tin-roof, tar-paper, and board shack, a few minutes later, squatting off among the trees to their left.

"Expect we'd best hole up in that shack for a spell," he said, nodding to Seela. The rain had aroused the girl, and she was now sitting rigidly erect in her saddle. "We'll make ourselves real comfortable in there — maybe just stay there till morning."

Fear registered through the weariness showing in Seela Clancy's eyes. She looked about hopefully as they swung toward the old cabin.

"You thinking that posse's around?" Cooter said with a laugh. "Hell, girl, it's time you forgot about them. If there ever was one, we done sidetracked them for good. You're my gal now, and there ain't nothing or nobody ever going to change that."

Drawing to a halt at the side of the cabin, Cooter dismounted, tied the horses to a

147

nearby pine, and then releasing Seela's hands from the horn, lifted her off the saddle.

"Going to be real cozy in there for me and you," he said, taking her by the arm and moving toward the door. The rain was coming down steadily and water was running off the brim of his hat in a small stream. "Yes sir, real cozy. Just you wait — you'll see."

The cabin had evidently been deserted for years. Dust and pack rat litter covered its floor, and as they entered, two of the small rodents scurried away and disappeared through a hole in the back wall. There was a leak in the roof and water was dripping noisily onto the rough plank floor.

"We best keep over on this side where we won't get no wetter," Cooter said, pointing to a dry area in the cabin. "I'm promising you here and now this'll be the last time you'll ever have to put up with a mess like this. You know why?"

Back to the wall, Seela settled onto the dusty planking. Her eyes were still filled with fear, and her young face was drawn and pale.

"No — I —"

"Just this — I'm rich now! Means you're rich, too, long as you stick with me."

Cooter pulled the saddlebags from his shoulder and patted the bulging pockets. "You see that? It's money, lots of it! More'n me and you'll need for a long time."

"The money — from the bank?"

"That's right, little lady, thirty thousand dollars! I ain't never seen that much cash, and I'm betting you ain't either. Hell, most cash I ever had at one time was maybe a hundred dollars.

"I come from poor folks, the kind that never had nothing — but that ain't the way it's going to be for me! I'm a rich man now, and me and you are going to have us a grand time riding around the country, seeing things and doing things we've always hankered to do." Dave Cooter paused. Eyes alight, he squatted before the girl. "We'll be doing all them things if you'll straighten up, act like you want to be my woman, and quit sniveling and bawling about it. It just ain't going to be no fun making you be my woman — you got to want it, too."

Seela's shoulders moved slightly. "I — I don't know . . . I just know I can't and I —"

"You mean you won't, and what you're wanting is to go home to your ma and pa. Well, forget them. I can give you more now than you ever hankered for!"

149

"But I —"

"But what?" Dave Cooter cut in as he unbuckled one of the saddlebag pouches. "Just you take a gander at all of this cash and tell me —"

The outlaw's words broke off abruptly as he spilled the contents of the pouch onto the floor — a box of cartridges, some articles of clothing, a sack of tobacco. Frowning, he turned to the other pouch, freed its straps from their buckles and emptied it onto the dusty floor alongside the pile from the other.

"Goddamnit!" Cooter exploded, staring at the items — a sack of coffee beans, a handful of jerky wrapped in a bit of paper, a yellow-paged magazine, and several other articles of no particular note.

"I've done got the wrong saddlebags!" the outlaw shouted, rising to his feet and beginning to pace back and forth agitatedly. "That damn Jube must've used another pair. Damn him to hell — I might've known something like this would have happened to me! I ain't never had no good luck — never have and never will! I been snake bit all of my sonofabitching life!"

Cooter paused, his face livid with anger, his hands clenching and unclenching as he glanced wildly about. After a few moments, he looked down at the girl.

"One damned thing for sure, since you're all I'm getting out of this messed-up fandango, I sure aim to take all I want of you!"

CHAPTER 16

Cole Dagget threw a glance over his shoulder as he reached a clump of scrub brush near a stand of trees. Josh Williams was only a stride behind and a bit to one side of him. His rifle was leveled at Cole's midsection, ready to fire. Pete, grasping the bridle of the buckskin, was following closely.

"Ain't no need to go looking back," Williams said, gesturing with a weapon. "That fellow and the little gal are probably long gone by now. Anyways, you can forget about her or any other gal 'cause we're turning you over to the sheriff for murder."

Dagget shrugged. He had not seen Cooter or Seela Clancy, but he did get a glimpse of the trail that led up the mountain that they would be taking.

"You're making a hell of a mistake," he said wearily. "That man's an outlaw. He was in on the robbing of the bank in Solitude. The girl's the daughter of a family named

Clancy who live there — she was working in the bank. The outlaws grabbed her and —"

"Sure, sure," Williams said as they veered toward a somewhat larger cabin a few yards to the left, "and ducks don't know how to swim! You just keep walking, mister, else we'll be turning you over to the sheriff dead. I don't reckon it'd make any difference to him . . . Now, step up and open that door, then go inside. Want you to raise up your hands and keep them up. Sure don't want you trying something cute."

Dagget did as he was directed and, mounting the small board landing that fronted the cabin, halted before the door. Pressing the thumb latch that held the thick panel shut, he pushed it open and moved inside, his mind searching madly for a way out of the predicament he was in. Unless he could get away from the two miners and overtook Cooter and Seela Clancy, he feared the worst for the girl.

"Set yourself down there in that chair," Williams ordered gruffly, and then as his partner entered the cabin, added, "Get some of them short ropes out of that box over there in the corner, Pete. I aim to tie this jasper up till we can find time to take him to the sheriff."

Pete crossed to the back of the room where several shovels, picks, and other tools were stacked and, reaching into an old ammunition box, obtained several pieces of rope. Returning with them, he began at once to tie Dagget to the chair, first pulling Cole's arms behind the furniture's straight, wooden back, and linking his wrists together, and then securing his ankles to the legs of the crudely built piece.

"I reckon that'll hold him," Pete said, stepping back and rubbing his palms together. "How'll we get him to the sheriff? Like that young fellow said, there just could be a big, fat reward for him."

"Ain't got everything figured out yet, but I'm working on it," Williams replied, leaning back against a wall. Outside it had grown darker as clouds began to fill the sky. "First off, we best have us a talk with Abe Parsons, see if he'll loan us his team and wagon. We can then truss up this bird, throw him in the back, and light out for town without no big to-do."

"I don't know about that," Pete said doubtfully. "Abe'll be wanting some of the reward."

"Wanting and getting's two different things. I'll tell you what — get a-straddle of that buckskin this fellow's riding and go see

Abe. Tell him the horse is his for the loan of his team and wagon."

"Now, that's a right smart idea," Pete declared with a toothy smile. "I'll head out for Abe's right now and see if I can strike a bargain with him. Expect I'll be back in about a half hour or so."

Josh Williams nodded. "Don't make it no longer if you can help it. Maybe we can get started for town yet this afternoon."

Dagget, listening in silence, watched Pete leave the cabin and cross to where the buckskin stood and, as Josh turned, walked leisurely to the rear of the room where a small cookstove stood, and began to stir something simmering in a pot, Dagget began to work feverishly at the rope binding his wrists. He had managed to create a small amount of slack by keeping his fists clenched, thus forcing his wrists apart, while Pete was tying them together.

A coffee pot on the stove began to rumble, and the odors coming from the stew and the chicory-laced drink reached Dagget and aroused hunger pangs in him, but he pushed the need aside; he had more important matters to worry about — getting away from the two miners and going after Cooter and the girl.

That purpose had dominated his mind

since the encounter at the camp, and he had come to fully realize what the girl was facing. The horse deal at Mangas Springs, so important to him earlier, had receded into the back of his mind, and other thoughts of his future — the ranch in Texas, his hopes of marrying Beth Lockhart, had all given way to concern for Seela Clancy. But he would be able to do nothing about any of it unless he found a way to escape from Josh Williams and his grizzled partner, Pete.

Cole continued to put pressure on the rope that lashed his wrists as he watched Williams pour himself a cup of coffee and sit down at a makeshift table. The rope was loosening, but there still wasn't enough slack to allow him to pull one hand free of the loop.

Suddenly he remembered the money in his saddlebags, the thirty thousand dollars that belonged to the Solitude bank. If Pete or Williams took it in mind to look inside the leather pouches, they would see the cash and be all the more convinced that he was an outlaw — the bank robber. Too, they could cave in to temptation, rid themselves of him, and keep the money for themselves.

"You'll be wasting your time taking me to the sheriff," he said, working steadily at the rope. "I'm a horse dealer, not an outlaw, and I can prove it."

"Could be," Williams said laconically, "but I reckon me and Pete'll just wait and see. We ain't doing nothing much right now, anyway."

"Be a long ride for nothing," Cole continued. One hand was almost loose. In another few minutes, both would be free. Then would come the problem of what best to do next. Whatever, it must be done before Pete returned. The two miners together, both strong, husky, work-hardened men, seasoned by endless days of laboring with pick and shovel, would be impossible to handle unless he could somehow get a gun — a hope further hindered by his bound ankles.

Dagget glanced about. Pete had taken his six-gun and was carrying it in his belt. The rifle Josh Williams used was propped against the wall just inside the doorway where the miner had left it.

Cole felt his left hand come free. He locked his fingers together instantly to prevent the rope from falling to the floor and attracting Williams's attention. Turning his head slightly, he glanced through the open doorway to the low hills and flats in the broad valley outside. There was no sign of Pete, as yet, but it wouldn't be long — he'd be gone for about a half hour, the miner had said. Dagget turned his attention to Josh Williams.

"You reckon I could have a cup of coffee and a little of that stew? Been more than a day since I ate."

Williams seemed to pay no attention to Dagget's request but continued to stare at a miner's supply company calendar on the wall opposite him. And then abruptly he stirred.

"Can't see why not," Williams said, setting his coffee on the table, "but I ain't trusting you none — I'll hold the cup."

"Suits me," Cole said. He had no plan of action in mind; he would simply meet the moment of opportunity if and when it came.

Josh Williams got to his feet, his broad, dark features set to expressionless lines and planes. Turning to the stove, he took a tin cup off an adjacent shelf, filled it with chicory coffee from the pot, and crossed to where Dagget was seated, ankles bound to the legs of the chair, arms still apparently linked together behind the rigid back of the crude piece of furniture.

"Ain't red hot," Williams said, and put the cup to Dagget's lips.

Cole's left hand came around fast. It connected with the cup of liquid, sent it sailing across the room. In that same instant, his knotted right fist drove solidly into the miner's jaw.

Williams yelled as he went down. Dagget, seeing the man was still conscious, rocked backward, stretched out an arm and snatched up the rifle. He had barely got his hands on the weapon when Williams regained his feet and came charging toward him. Grasping the rifle by the barrel, Cole swung at the miner's head. The stock made a solid, thudding sound and splintered when it crashed into Williams's skull, dropping the miner to the floor like a sack of grain.

Hurriedly, Dagget dug into his pocket for the jackknife he carried. Pete would be showing up soon, and he must be free of the damned chair to deal with him. Opening the large blade of the knife, he slashed the rope binding his ankles and crossed quickly to where Williams lay. Josh was out cold and would remain so for some time. A hard grin pulled at Dagget's mouth as he moved toward the door. Earlier, Williams had been real generous, jabbing him in the back with the rifle; it was only fitting that he got a taste of the weapon's opposite end.

Reaching the doorway, Cole looked off in the direction Pete had taken. He drew back hastily. The miner, astride the buckskin and having trouble keeping the horse to the slow lope, was only a dozen yards away.

Wheeling, Dagget seized Williams by the feet and dragged him off to one side where he would not be immediately visible. Crossing then to the open doorway, he took up a position against the wall just within the entrance. Moments later, he heard the miner draw up in front of the cabin and, muttering something under his breath, dismount. Seconds later, there was the creaking of boards as the man stepped up onto the landing.

"Abe weren't there," he said. "Had gone up to the new diggings, Charley Taw said, and —"

Dagget seized the man by the arm as he came through the doorway and, pivoting on a heel, swung him hard into the adjacent wall. Dishes, pans, and other articles on a shelf nearby clattered noisily to the floor, and Pete, his breath leaving him in a single, gusty blast, went down without uttering another word.

Dagget drew his .45 from the unconscious man's belt and slid it back into its holster. He had a fleeting inclination to pour himself another cup of coffee and help himself to a few mouthfuls of the stew that was bubbling on the stove, but it was only a thought. The sooner he got on the trail of Dave Cooter and Seela Clancy, the better. He reckoned he could stand being hungry for a while longer.

CHAPTER 17

Losing no time, Dagget hurried into the open and mounted the weary buckskin. He couldn't expect much from the horse, he realized; the gelding had enjoyed very little rest since leaving Solitude. Glancing up to the overcast sky, Cole cut away from the cabin where Williams and Pete lay and pointed for the trail carving a path up the side of the nearby slope.

It was slow going, made doubly so by the buckskin's worn condition, but the animal plodded gamely on, never slowing on the somewhat steep course, but maintaining a steady pace. An hour or so later, rain began to fall, and although it was only a light shower, it did make the path up the mountainside slippery and Dagget again don his poncho.

Several times he brought the horse to a stop, dismounted, and walked ahead of the animal to give him rest. This cost him time and increased the frustration that gripped him, but there was nothing he could do about it. Better to use care where the buckskin was concerned than end up with a horse suffering a broken leg.

But he felt he was fortunate in one way, considering it wasn't one of the fierce summer rainstorms that periodically lashed the mountains, filling the arroyos and gullies and sending them racing down the slopes carrying rocks, trees, soil, and debris with them. However, there was no guarantee the shower would not resolve into that kind of storm, and the worry of that lodged in the back of Dagget's mind and hung there.

He tried to estimate just how far ahead Dave Cooter and the girl might be — at least an hour, he reckoned, but there was no way of being sure. They could have halted to rest, or possibly the outlaw had turned off the narrow path and had taken a route across the side of the mountain. His being certain was not the case, so Cole began to watch the trail for the tracks of the two horses.

They were not easy to find as the path was overgrown and studded with rocks. The shower, too, coming as it did after the outlaw and Seela had passed, was complicating matters. But now and then Cole did find evidence of their passage and that kept him moving steadily on.

He hoped the Clancy girl was still all right. Except for the weariness that weighed upon her due to the continual riding since her abduction in Solitude, she appeared to have been unharmed. That Cooter had been rough with her for some reason had also been apparent. However, Dagget thought, Seela Clancy should be thankful that they had been unable to halt for any length of time.

Leading the buckskin over the treacherous ground, Cole plodded doggedly on through the thin shower. Matters had really gone wrong for him, he thought, just when everything had been looking bright. True, he had recovered his eight hundred dollars, but without a doubt he was losing the best horse deal he had ever encountered. Worst of all, it threw a kink in his long-delayed plans insofar as marrying Beth Lockhart was concerned.

Dagget swore deeply as he thought of Beth. He had looked forward to starting out the year with her as his wife. Now he would have to explain to her why they must wait a time longer — wait until he could turn up another good deal that would enable him to get into raising and breeding horses properly.

Beth would protest and declare that his starting out with little more than nothing didn't matter — and he knew she would mean it. Beth was that kind of woman, but he had sworn an oath to himself soon after they met that while he wanted her in the worst way, he would never marry her until he was in a position to provide her with a comfortable house and a decent way of living.

Ranch life was hard for a woman at best. He had seen too many wives during his drifting about the country who were old and worn out long before their time. He vowed he'd never let that happen to Beth.

Cole recalled how she had looked that day when he had ridden out. Standing on the long porch of her father's ranch house, she had had her dark hair gathered on the top of her head, and her blue eyes showed sadness at his leaving, her lips set in full, curving lines as she watched him go. Of slim figure, she had been wearing a pale blue suit with puffed sleeves, a lacy white shirtwaist, and a string tie, also of blue. He remembered, too, how her skirt had come down snugly over her hips, so sleek and trim-looking, and tipped the arch of her shoes.

Beth was not only a beautiful woman but a capable one as well. She came from good ranching stock and would make him an ideal companion if ever he could get squared away and marry her. He had long ago made his proposal and she had accepted, but he was beginning to wonder if Beth would wait much longer for him, and that doubt, when it occurred, always filled him with worry.

It was possible she didn't share his dream of raising horses as deeply as he. That she would, instead, prefer that he throw in with her father in running his vast Texas spread. Tom Lockhart was growing old and would welcome him, not only into the family, but as one who could take over the operation of the ranch and relieve him of the responsibility. And when the date came that —

A bird fluttered across the rough trail and disappeared into the dripping brush. The rain had stopped and Dagget noted that the hoofprints of Seela's and Clancy's horses were now clearly visible in the soft, dark soil. It could mean, he reasoned, that he was not far behind them.

Halting, Cole swung back into the saddle, cursing a bit as he settled onto the wet leather. The path was wider, if rockier, and he saw that he was getting near the crest of a ridge. A hundred yards or so later, he again drew to a stop. The path had come to a more definite and well-traveled trail, running at right angles. The Escondido Trail — there was no doubt about it. Dropping from the back of the buckskin, Dagget made certain of the tracks he was following. Cooter and his prisoner had turned right and were continuing on up the mountain.

Cole returned to his saddle and urged the buckskin into a slow walk. Cooter and the girl would be easier to follow on the better trail; one on which he could travel faster if the buckskin were not so worn. But the horses Seela and Dave Cooter were riding would be in no better condition; they, too, would be moving slowly.

Once more Cole halted, this time to look back down the trail for signs of the posse. He thought he had heard something off in the distance, but as he listened into the dripping hush, he could hear nothing. After a bit, he shrugged. That the posse would be on the trail and anywhere near was a long shot, one likely not to prove to be a fact.

Raking the buckskin with his spurs, he started the horse forward again. The trail was not particularly steep in that area as they were in a swale or saddle of sorts, just prior to the final climb to the crest, and the horse was having no difficulty. A canted, faded sign off to one side drew Dagget's attention. WASHOUT 5 MI. it stated, its crude arrow pointing on up the trail. Another of the many mining camps, probably deserted as were most of those to be found in the Mogollons and Sacramentos.

Cole pressed on, his weariness and hunger dragging at him with leaden insistence. The buckskin, too, was beginning to wear down, and Cole knew that soon he would have to call a halt and let the horse get a few hours rest — something he could use also.

Again, he came to a halt. The tracks of the two horses he was following had turned off the trail and were headed into the trees and brush to his left. It could mean only one thing; the horses that Cooter and the girl were riding were playing out also and needed to rest, otherwise Dave Cooter would never risk stopping but would keep going until he reached what he considered a safe hiding place.

Leaving the trail, Dagget, his eyes on the deeply imprinted tracks in the soft, muddy ground, headed into the trees. While the shower had ceased, the sky still clung to a thick overcast which made it difficult at times in the murky grayness to follow the hoofprints among the densely growing pines and brush. Dagget kept at it, however, doubling back and forth at times when he lost the tracks, ignoring the soaking he was getting from rain-laden branches that slapped at him while he stuck, stubbornly, to the task of trailing the outlaw and the girl who continued to bear southward.

A half hour later, with the rain beginning to come down again, Dagget drew up at the edge of a small clearing. On its far side stood a weathered old board shack, its steeply slanted tin roof and bleached plank walls looming grayly through the shower. Tied to a nearby tree, hipshot, heads hanging low, were two horses. One was Dave Cooter's black and brown pinto, the other was Fowler's bay that Seela Clancy was riding.

CHAPTER 18

"There's smoke a-coming up from the yonder side of that ridge to the north," Conroy said, pulling to a halt in front of Brinkman and the rest of the posse. "Ain't no way of telling if it's a camp or some miner's shack."

At Brinkman's direction, Conroy and Ben Wilk had swung away from the Escondido Trail to have a look at the country lying to the north.

"Ain't no cabins over there," Ed Speakman said, "unless they just been built in the last month or two."

"I'm betting it's them, then," John Clancy said. The early morning air was cold and he had pulled on the heavy mackinaw he'd worn for years when mining. "Let's get right over there."

"Could be only a couple of miners or drifters making a night camp," Brinkman said, his features almost obscured by the steamy cloud of breath coming from his mouth as he spoke. "Might be smarter for us to split up and —"

"Do as you goddamn well please — I'm riding over to have me a look!" Clancy snapped, and, spurring his horse, swung off the trail. "You coming?" he called back to Conroy.

Conroy glanced at Brinkman as if for confirmation. The tall miner-turned-rancher shrugged.

"As well we all go," he said resignedly. "Speakman tells me we can cut back to the main trail just about anywhere in these hills."

Speakman nodded as the posse turned to follow Conroy and John Clancy. "Well, there ain't but two or three trails leading out of this part of the country. And they all head back south and join up with the Escondido."

"We best spread out," Brinkman said a time later when they halted on a rocky hogback. "That smoke's coming from just west of that hill. Let's play it smart and circle in."

Clancy, with Conroy at his side, swore impatiently. "Like I said — do as you please. We're heading straight in."

"Use your head, John — they'll hear you coming and be gone before you get there,"

Brinkman cautioned.

"Maybe," Clancy shot back, "and just maybe they won't."

Brinkman swore and for the first time showed signs of losing patience. "Damn it all, John, I'm as anxious to catch up with that bunch as you are — but we've got to go at it right or we never will! Now if you —"

He broke off his words as Clancy, unhearing and heedless, spurred off in the direction of the smoke. After a bit, Pete Odle broke the silence.

"You got to sort of overlook the way he's acting, Mr. Brinkman. He's mighty fearful over that girl of his."

"We all are," the rancher replied, "but chasing out over these flats and hills like John's wanting to do could mean losing track of those outlaws altogether." He shifted his attention to Speakman, sitting hunched in his saddle, hands tucked into his armpits for warmth.

"You sure about all the trails around here leading back to the Escondido?"

"Sure am, unless somebody's come along and blazed out a couple of new ones."

"Not much chance of that," Jim Fontane said.

"Then we might as well go along with

172

Clancy. If this turns out to be another snipe hunt, we can cut back to the main trail. My belief is that those outlaws are heading for the other side of the mountain — and then on to Arizona."

"Be my guess, too," Odle said as the riders cut about and left the ridge. "It's a hell of a long way to anything if a man heads north."

"A long way to anywhere," Fontane commented glumly.

With Brinkman and Pete Odle in the lead, the party rode on, following in the tracks of John Clancy and Dave Conroy, now a half mile ahead in the distance. When they were near the hill beyond which the wisps of smoke were rising, Brinkman motioned for the men with him to spread out and approach the far side of the hill from different points.

"Doubt if it'll make any difference with Clancy and Conroy riding straight in like they are," Odle said, glancing skyward. "Something's drawing buzzards."

Brinkman followed Odle's glance. Two big, broad-winged scavengers had begun to circle above the area beyond the hill. Off to the east, three more of their kind were drifting lazily in.

"Something's caught their attention for

sure," Brinkman said. He knew what the others were thinking — that it might be Seela Clancy dead or left to die by the outlaws, a possibility none of them was willing to voice. "Could be a deer or maybe an antelope killed by a big cat."

"Probably," Fontane agreed, "but we best get over there quick and find out."

At once the men broke their mounts into a brisk trot over the uneven ground and quickly reached the opposite side of the hill.

"Here's two of them outlaws," Conroy called. "Been gunned down. They're deader'n doornails."

Brinkman rode up to where the general store owner was standing beside one of the bodies. "Any sign of the girl?" he asked, and then to Odle, "Take a look around, Pete."

Conroy shook his head. "Nope, but John's out there beating the bushes — and scared to death what he'll find."

Brinkman swore softly and dismounted. The other posse members were climbing down from their horses too, setting up a dry creaking of leather and grunting in relief as they left their saddles.

"These are the two that seemed to be bossing the hold up," Speakman said, looking down at the sagging, gray features of Jube Fowler and Apache Reed. "Wonder where the other'n is."

"I'd guess he shot it out with these two and then took off with the money — and John's girl," Ben Wilk said. "Ain't nothing strange about that — just wanted it all for himself."

"Don't forget about that other jasper — Dagget, the one that was in the bank too. He'll be with them."

"Right," Speakman said. "Dagget and the young one that snatched up the Clancy girl are in this together — you can bet on it. Expect that they were waiting for him. He got here where they'd made camp, then either they got to quarreling among themselves over the girl or the money, or both, with the two young ones on one side, these two on the other. The young ones came out on top and took off."

Brinkman listened in silence. It was beginning to look as if the man named Dagget was in with the outlaws after all, but for some reason he could not understand, he was finding it hard to believe.

"Looks like the fire they had going sort of got away from them," Fontane commented, staring at the lengthy strip of dark ashes and scorched ground. "Wind must've blown to beat hell."

"Was one horse standing here when we

rode up," Conroy said. "Didn't find nothing in the saddlebags worth looking at. Expect they put Clancy's girl on the other'n so's they could travel faster . . . Here comes Clancy back. Looks like he didn't find nothing."

Clancy, a paleness showing through the brown of his leathery skin, pulled to a halt before the men. "Couldn't find no sign of her," he said heavily. "I reckon they've still got her with them."

"Means she's still alive, John," Speakman said gently. "You ought to be glad of that."

"I ain't so sure," Clancy replied slowly. "Them bastards could've used her — and being only sixteen — well, she just might be better off if she was dead."

"That's no way to look at it," Brinkman said sternly. "It'll be wrong to give up on her till we know for sure."

"Who the hell's giving up?" Clancy demanded. "Just telling you how things look." He paused, brushed at his mouth with a gloved hand. "I aim to keep right on hunting until I find her."

"What we all intend to do," Brinkman said. "You figure out which way they went when they left here?"

"There's a trail on the other side of that creek," Clancy answered with a wave of his hand. "Only one leading out of here, near as I could see."

"Probably the one they used," Brinkman agreed. He hesitated and turned as Pete Odle rode up. "Anything?"

Odle shook his head. "Not much. Them two stiffs was killed over in the brush, then dragged up here by the fire. Was somebody else setting over there by that little hill near the creek — with the girl."

"You saying there were two of them here while a third one and my girl were over there by themselves?" Clancy asked in a strained voice.

"Way it looks, Mr. Clancy —"

John Clancy lowered his head and swore deeply. The breath of the men and the horses still hung in the cold, motionless air in small white clouds about their heads.

"You know for sure which way they went, Pete, after they left here?" he said a few moments later. "It be my daughter and them other two outlaws."

"Two?" Odle repeated, pushing his hat back and running stubby fingers through his hair.

"John figures the one that got hit over the head in the bank — Dagget — is one of them, and that they waited for him here," Brinkman explained. "Was a shoot-out and then the two men rode off with John's daughter."

"Could be," Odle said. "Never got down and looked at that trail good. Know there was horses on it."

"Then, for God's sake, let's get moving!" Clancy said in a desperate voice. "Longer we wait, the farther ahead they'll get!"

"Got to bury these two. Outlaws or not, they deserve —"

"The hell with them," Clancy shouted. "Let the buzzards and the coyotes do the burying!"

"Just can't do that," Ben Wilk said. "Wouldn't be decent. I don't like pulling out on you, John, but I've got responsibilities in town. I'll stay and put them under, then head on back."

"Can figure on me to help, Ben," Fontane said. "Expect they're needing me back home, too."

"Go on, go on," Clancy said impatiently. "Hell, all of you go on back! I can run them killers down by myself — don't need none of you! Means you, too, Brinkman!"

"The rest of us aren't pulling out on you, John. It's only Ben and Fontane," the rancher said, glancing around.

Ed Speakman nodded. Odle and Conroy did likewise. Clancy hawked and spat into the weeds. Overhead, clouds were beginning to assemble.

"Sure we're staying," Speakman said, raising his eyes to the sky. "Looks like rain's a-coming."

"Let it," Clancy snapped, and cutting out across the flat, headed for the slope where Pete Odle had seen tracks.

At once the others crossed to their horses and mounted. Brinkman paused beside Fontane and Wilk.

"You've got no tools to dig with," he said. "Was I you two, I'd drag the bodies over the closest gully, and throw a lot of rocks and brush on them. That'll keep the buzzards and maybe the coyotes from bothering them."

"We was wondering how we'd get them buried," Wilk said. "I reckon that's the answer."

"When you get back to town," Brinkman said, "you might tell Mrs. Clancy that we're still tracking those outlaws and that far as we know her daughter is still all right."

"Sure thing," Fontane said. "We'll tell her."

Settling himself squarely in his saddle, Brinkman hurried to catch up with the other riders. He could see John Clancy now at the foot of the mountain on the far side of the creek. His one-time partner was on foot, walking his horse slowly along its bank before climbing the trail that wound in and out of the brush and rocks. Brinkman wished Clancy would hold back and allow Odle to take the lead. Pete would not just follow the trail itself but would depend on the tracks left by the horses to guide him. It was entirely possible the outlaws would turn off the trail at some point.

He'd not say anything to Clancy about it, however. It was Clancy's posse and John would run it as he saw fit. Already, they had come to words over making a couple of decisions which, Brinkman supposed, were Clancy's right to make alone.

But Seela was Lorena's daughter and Harry Brinkman felt an obligation somehow to find the girl as quickly as possible, which explained his attempts to take the shortest and most logical course that he felt the outlaws might pursue. He was hoping and praying they would find the girl unharmed, but he was far from convinced that such would be the case. In the hands of one, if not two hardened outlaws, she likely would not fare very well — particularly if they halted for any length of time.

Brinkman was still unsure about the man named Dagget, that he actually was a member of the outlaw bunch. Somehow he hadn't had the look of a criminal, and Brinkman prided himself on his ability to judge men.

The morning wore on and soon they dropped off into a gentle valley where several cabins sat in a clearing. The nearest one appeared deserted, but Odle, restlessly searching back and forth, halted at the next in the irregular row, lying beyond a spur of trees to the north.

It was being lived in, but there was no one around, Pete reported to Brinkman and the others. Likely the occupants were off in the hills somewhere working their claims at that hour of the day.

The first spatter of rain struck them as they started up the slope beyond the shacks. Odle had moved into the lead, with Clancy directly behind him.

"Damn rain's going to wipe out them tracks sure as hell," he grumbled a few minutes later as they wound their way up the slope.

"Sure ain't going to argue that," Pete replied. "But the way I see it, no man's getting off this trail unless he's got hisself a pair of wings. Brush and rocks've got it hemmed in tight."

They rode on through the intermittent

showers, the path bearing southwest and climbing steadily toward a high, misty rim well in the distance. Twice Odle called a halt, dismounted, and got down to examine the trail despite his one belief that turning off would be an impossibility. Each time he found the hoofprints — those of three horses — that he was searching for. It was slow going in places also, forcing the riders to dismount and lead their horses — a necessity that irritated John Clancy and set him to fretting over the delay.

And then an hour or so after crossing a particularly bad section of the mountain's side, and with the rain coming down harder, the path ended at the edge of a fairly wide and much better trail.

"Just what I was telling you — that cow path we been following circled right back to the Escondido Trail," Speakman said. "They all do. We could've saved time if we'd've kept on it instead of sashaying off into the hills like we done."

"Second guessing's always mighty easy," Conroy said. Water was running off the brim of his hat in several places and sliding down the smooth surface of the yellow slicker he had pulled on. "Point is, what do we do now?"

"Just what I'm wondering," Speakman

said. "Them outlaws could've turned back when they got to here."

Brinkman waited for Clancy to speak, and when the man failed to make himself heard, he said, "Not likely. They wouldn't head for Solitude — and that's where this road will take them —"

"There, and to the forks where they could keep going north to Socorro," Speakman said.

Water was coursing off him and all the others — running off their hat brims to fall on their slickers and drip to the ground. Sitting there in the gray gloom of the storm, they glistened like yellow wraiths.

Again Brinkman waited for Clancy to comment, but his onetime partner remained silent and seemingly uncertain what to do. Concern and fear for Seela were apparently having their strong way with him.

"Not apt to do that either," Brinkman said finally. "They're bound to know there's a posse on their tail. I'd expect them to keep going up the mountain, cross over, and keep running for Arizona."

"Sure is what I'd be doing," Pete Odle agreed.

"Ain't there no tracks that'll tell what they done?" Speakman asked, turning to Odle.

"Nope. Rain's done took care of them.

Now I —"

The distant hollow sound of gunshots coming from farther up the trail reached them through the slackening rain. The fear in John Clancy's eyes heightened.

"By God — I'll bet that's them!" he yelled. "And they're fighting over my girl!"

"Now, John," Speakman said as Clancy spurred out onto the trail. "It could just be somebody shooting a cat or a bear. You can't —"

"I aim to find out!" Clancy shouted over his shoulder and, hunched low in his saddle, struck off up the trail.

At once, the others cut in behind him and, stringing out in a short line, followed.

CHAPTER 19

Slumped in his saddle on the buckskin, ignoring the water dripping off his hat, and with the good smell of wet pines in his nostrils, Cole Dagget studied the shack. It did not appear to be one of the plentiful abandoned structures that dotted the slopes of the Sacramentos and Mogollons as he had first thought, but it looked to be lived in.

There was firewood stacked against one wall with a discarded piece of tin laid upon its top to ward off snow and rain; a small vegetable garden was to the south of it; and several pieces of clothing hung from a line running from one corner of the cabin to a nearby tree.

The thought came to Dagget that while the place had a regular occupant, in all likelihood that person was absent at the time and Cooter and Seela Clancy had taken advantage of that fact and moved in.

Or another good possibility was the owner, being there, had opposed the outlaw and he had then forcibly taken possession.

In either case, he had caught up with Cooter and the kidnapped Seela Clancy. His next move was to free the girl. Veering off into the trees east of the cabin, Cole circled the clearing and came upon the structure on its windowless, blind side. Dismounting, he tethered the buckskin to a stump a dozen strides below the cabin and the two horses tied up near its corner.

The rain had all but stopped, and shedding the slicker, Dagget lifted his gun from the holster, checked it briefly, and then let it drop back into place. That done, he made his way quietly over the water-soaked ground to the front of the building.

Halting beside the door he cautiously tested the thumb latch. It gave readily, allowing the panel to open a crack. The sound of Cooter's voice, low and insistent, reached him. He would have no problem entering the cabin, that was evident, but first it would be smart to have a look inside, to see what he would be up against. Staying close to the wall of the cabin, Cole moved to the window in the front of the structure and immediately adjacent to the door. The streaked glass glistened wetly in the weak sunlight struggling to break through the heavy clouds. Reaching it, Dagget pulled off his hat and peered into the cluttered room.

Cooter was rummaging about among several sacks and tins of food on a shelf to the left. Seela Clancy was slumped on a chair nearby staring vacantly at the small cookstove an arm's length away. She was wearing a jacket that the outlaw had given her, but she appeared soaked to the skin and the torn yellow dress she wore was plastered to her body. Seela was close to complete exhaustion, and as she raised her head to glance at Cooter, the weariness that dragged at her features gave her a much older look.

"Can't we go on?" Cole heard her ask in a faint voice. Despite the fatigue she was hoping to keep moving rather than stay for any length of time in the cabin with Cooter. "It's stopped raining — and maybe there'll be a town —"

"We'll do real fine right here," the outlaw replied. "There's plenty of grub, and resting up till morning will do us both a lot of good. That'll suit you, won't it?"

Seela shook her head helplessly. "I — I don't know. I'm so tired I only want —"

"Told you before, it ain't what you want that you'll be getting from here on, but what

I want!" Angry, he turned to the stove, lifted one of the lids, and began to poke impatiently at the damp wood that was slow in burning. "This damned fire — if it don't start up pretty quick, I'm busting up that table so's I'll have some dry firewood!"

The girl murmured something that Dagget failed to hear, but it brought Cooter about once more.

"Now, I've had enough of your whining and bawling! I want you to get out of them wet clothes and then crawl into that bunk. Hear?"

Seela shook her head and pulled the jacket closer about her young body. Cooter resumed his problem with the fire. After a few moments he looked up.

"You're going to catch your death setting around in those wet duds," he warned.

Seela continued to resist the outlaw's order, simply remaining where she was, huddled on the chair while water dripped slowly from her clothing. The outlaw finally got the fire going and turned his attention then to the food supply lined up on the shelf, and with his attention thus occupied, and his back to the window and door, Dagget resumed a careful scrutiny of the room.

It would be easy to simply burst into the cabin and shoot it out with Cooter, but if the outlaw put up any resistance, it could endanger Seela. Dagget could make use of the stove himself, use it as protection, and he figured that most likely Cooter then would throw himself in behind the heavy table and chair that stood on the opposite side of the room.

It would be close, but if he could get the girl to drop to the floor, there was a good chance she would not get hurt. Whatever happened, he had to do something. Seela was suffering from exposure and fear, and she had to get out of the rain-soaked clothes she was wearing into something dry. But even more he understood the girl's determination not to do as Cooter had directed — an order that no doubt would become an enforced command as soon as the outlaw got his cooking chores out of the way.

Drawing his gun, Dagget moved silently back to the door. Masking the click of the hammer as he cocked the weapon with a cupped hand, he took a deep breath, raised a booted foot, and drove it into the thick board panel.

The door swung in with a splintering sound. Seela screamed and half rose from her chair. Dagget barely heard or saw. His attention was on Dave Cooter. The outlaw, in the act of filling a fire-stained coffee pot from a water bucket, pivoted. As Dagget rushed in, the outlaw threw the water into his face. Cole, blinded momentarily, halted. In the next instant, the coffee pot crashed into the gun in his hand. Numbed fingers released their grip on the weapon and it fell to the floor with a thud.

As Seela's continuing screams filled the cabin and echoed in his ears, Cole, recovering fast, threw himself on the outlaw, pinning the man's arms to his sides before he could get at his own weapon, and driving him back against the wall. Dishes and pans rattled and a framed picture standing on the shelf fell to the floor with a crash.

"Goddamn you!" Cooter gasped. "I'll —"

Dagget jerked back and drove his fist into the outlaw's belly. Cooter buckled, then rocked to one side, avoiding the fist that Dagget brought up from his heels. Cooter twisted away, his hand clawing for the gun still in the holster on his hip. Dagget knocked the outlaw's hand aside and, heaving and sucking hard for breath, sent another blow into Cooter's middle, but Dagget was off balance and there was little power in his fist.

Cooter tripped suddenly as they wrestled back and forth in each other's grasp. The outlaw went down hard with Dagget on top.

For several moments, they thrashed about on the dusty, half-muddy floor, flailing at each other ineffectively, and then Dagget broke free and rolled clear. He felt the hard, unyielding shape of his dropped weapon under his body. Twisting about, he hurriedly snatched up the gun and bounded to his feet.

In that fraction of a moment, Cooter fired. At such close range, the bullet, striking Dagget in the thigh, drove him back against the wall.

"Get down!" he yelled at Seela Clancy as he sank to the floor and hurriedly dragged himself in behind the stove.

With smoke and echoes that overrode Seela's screaming filling the room, Cole snapped a shot at Cooter, now crouched behind the table and the overturned chair. The outlaw triggered an answering bullet that missed and buried itself in the wall behind Dagget. As the smoke trapped in the room thickened, Cooter half rose and started for the better shelter offered by the bunk.

Dagget fired quickly at the darting, shadowy figure and missed. Steadying himself as pain stabbed through his body, Cole fired his .45 again. The outlaw rocked back as the bullet drove into him. He recovered instantly and now, on hands and knees, began to move away through the thickening screen of smoke.

Keeping low, conscious of the warm feeling of blood oozing from his wound and trickling slowly down his leg, Dagget worked his way from the stove toward the opposite side of the room. Again, Cooter fired and once more Cole felt the searing, shocking impact of a bullet driving into his arm.

He sank to the floor, his senses waning and strength slowly ebbing. Stretched full length, he strained to get a glimpse of the outlaw through the haze. The outlaw triggered another shot. The bullet was wild and went to Cole's left, striking the stove or something else metallic, and went screaming off into the cabin.

Dagget lay motionless hoping for one more chance at the outlaw before he blacked out. It was quiet. The echoes had died and Seela Clancy was no longer screaming. Somewhere close by was Dave Cooter. He wanted to hear the outlaw move or get a glimpse of him through the bluish, choking haze.

Almost at that same instant, Dagget saw the outlaw. He was down on hands and knees creeping toward the door. Suddenly cool, steadying himself by lying prone on the dusty floor, ignoring the pain that throbbed through him, Cole leveled his gun at Cooter and pressed off a shot. The cabin rocked again with the gunshot. Smoke bulged upward and echoes once more rebounded in the small room.

Through the thick pall, Dagget saw Cooter jolt and lurch to one side. The outlaw, a dim shape in the haze, drew himself up slightly. He raised his weapon. It wavered in his faltering hand. Dagget saw the muzzle flash as the outlaw got off a last, final shot and then felt the impact of a tremendous blow to the side of the head as a cloak of blackness swiftly enveloped him.

CHAPTER 20

"He's coming to —"

Dagget was only vaguely aware of the pain, of the voice, and of the other sounds in the room — people moving about, low-spoken conversation, the scuff of boots, the crackling of wood burning in the stove.

"Just too goddamn bad he ain't dead like the others. Would've saved us a lot of trouble."

Through the slowly clearing fog that shrouded his senses, it dawned on Cole that they were speaking about him. Somehow they had gotten the idea he was one of the outlaw bunch. Muttering, he glanced about.

He was lying on the floor. Two men were bending over him. One, an older individual with a tobacco-stained beard, had just finished wrapping a makeshift bandage around the wound in his arm, and having ripped the strip of cloth down its center, was now tying the opposing ends together.

His pants leg had been slit and the gunshot injury low in his thigh had already been attended to. There was a burning sensation along his left temple, and his head ached mightily.

"He'll live," the bearded man said. "Lost a pot full of blood, but that won't hurt him none. Neither will that wallop he took on the head. Bullet just grazed him."

The posse . . . It could only be the posse from Solitude. Cole lifted his head and looked about. He recognized Harry Brinkman and John Clancy. The four other men were strangers. The girl — where was she? Clancy and one of the men moved slightly and Dagget caught a glimpse of her. Seela was lying motionless on the table. There was a bandage around her head.

"I'm pulling out right now," Clancy's taut, anxious voice filled the quiet. "Just got to get her to town and Doc Welch quick as I can."

"We can take my wagon. It ain't much, but it'll be better'n you holding her in your saddle," one of the strangers, a tall, lean man in faded bib overalls and a coarse shirt, said. Likely he was the owner of the cabin, or else someone who happened by when the shooting started. Having a wagon ruled out the possibility of his being a member of the posse.

"Obliged," Clancy mumbled. "Like to borrow a couple of blankets too — and maybe a tarp in case it starts in raining again."

"Sure thing," the miner said. "Just take them off the bunk. I'll go out and fix a pallet in the wagon for her. I'll holler when it's ready and you can bring her out."

Clancy nodded woodenly. "Just got to get her to town — to Doc Welch —"

Somehow Seela had gotten hurt, Dagget realized. Most likely she bad been hit by a glancing bullet. She had not been in the line of fire, he was certain of that — he'd even warned her to keep down. Ignoring the pain, Dagget raised himself to a sitting position.

"Is the girl bad hurt?"

"Bad!" the bearded man echoed in a low voice. "One of you shot her in the head when you were fighting over her and the money."

"Neither one of us shot her — it was an accident, a stray bullet," Dagget said angrily. "And it wasn't the way you're putting it. I tracked them for miles — all the way to here —"

"Wagon's all ready," the miner called from beyond the doorway.

"John's leaving," one of the other members of the posse, a slim man in range clothing, said. "Best I give him a hand."

Turning, he crossed to the table, saying something to Clancy as he started to lift Seela's slight body. Clancy shook his head and slipping his hands under the girl took her into his arms. Carrying her as easily and tenderly as if she were an infant, he moved to the door and stepped outside where a light spring wagon had been drawn up.

"Good luck, John," the man who had been bending over Dagget assisting the bearded one in taking care of his wounds, called out, and then added in a low voice, "He's sure going to need all he can get. That girl's hurt real bad." He paused, glared at Dagget. "I sure would hate to be in your boots, mister, if that girl dies."

Cole made no reply, but watched as the wagon with the miner on the seat driving, and John Clancy in the bed holding Seela in his thick arms, rolled off toward the trail. Coming half around, he faced the quartet of men ranged before him in a half circle. He saw nothing but hate in the eyes of all but Harry Brinkman.

"It was an accident — far as I know. Told you that. And it wasn't a shoot-out over her."

"Sure, sure — of course not! You was trying to save her from your partner there."

"Yes, reckon you could say that's what I was doing — but that man lying dead over there was no partner of mine. His name's Cooter. Was him and two others that were partners. Names were Reed and Fowler. They're the ones that robbed the bank and took off with the girl."

"You kill them, too? We came across them bodies back there on a flat."

Dagget nodded. "Had no choice."

The bearded man shrugged. "Just a case of outlaws fighting among themselves for money they stole."

The younger man beside him nodded. "And for John Clancy's girl, don't forget that, Ed."

Anger pushed pain to the background in Cole Dagget. "Not that way at all! I'm no outlaw; I deal in horses. Name's Dagget and —"

"Don't go trying to squirm out of this," the tall man named Ed cut in. "We've got you dead to rights, mister."

"Let him talk," Harry Brinkman said. "Could be some truth in what he's saying."

"Truth?" the younger man echoed. "Hell, the truth couldn't be no plainer. We found the bank's money in the saddlebags of his horse. And we come across him and that jasper over there, here in the cabin with the Clancy girl — one dead and the other'n shot up. What more truth do you want?"

Brinkman brushed at the stubble showing on his chin and cheeks. "Could be he's trying to tell us he was following them — tracking them —"

"Ain't arguing that — he followed them after they left town so's he could join up with them again — just like John Clancy figured he done."

"No," Cole said flatly, "I was following them to get my money back."

"And then when you didn't like the split, you killed them two down on the flat. Cooter, there, probably seen what was in the wind and took off, and you had to chase him," the younger man finished, his tone filled with conviction.

"Not how it was at all," Dagget said stubbornly. His head continued to ache and the throbbing pains in his leg and arm had intensified, while the groove along his temple where Cooter's last bullet had grazed him felt as if it were on fire. "After I had it out with Reed and Fowler, I had a notion to ride on, then I realized I couldn't do that, couldn't turn my back on the girl, leave her in Cooter's hands."

"Yeah, I'll bet," Ed said scornfully.

"Just how it was," Dagget continued, hanging tight to his temper. "I rode off after them — built a big fire in hopes you would see it and follow. There were a couple of drifters or busted miners come along about the time I was leaving. They were headed south. I asked them if they ran into your posse to tell —"

"We never seen nobody, did we, Dave?" Ed said, shaking his head. "Any of the rest of you? How about you, Harry? You, Pete? Any of you meet any drifters or anybody else while we were coming here?"

The man in range clothing, evidently Pete, moved his head from side to side. So also did Dave, the younger man. Harry Brinkman, his face slack from weariness, his damp clothing hanging limply from his tall frame, stirred.

"No, can't say as I did. But there was that big fire that he said he set — sort of a signal."

"Maybe he set it and maybe he didn't," Dave said.

"Not likely anybody would build a campfire that big," Brinkman said indifferently. " 'Specially outlaws on the run. They'd not be fool enough to advertise where they were."

Dave spat into the nearby woodbox. "Could've been just a regular fire only the wind might've got up and it spread."

"Yeah, I suppose," Brinkman, tired of the argument, said wearily.

Dagget, fed up with the senseless bickering also, glanced through the doorway. The rain had stopped and the sun was shining brightly on the freshly washed land.

"Ain't it about time we was heading back for town?" Dave asked. "Be midnight by the time we can get there now — maybe later, figuring how beat the horses are."

"Could stay right here for the night," Pete said. "Good place to sleep, and we can borrow some of Jackson's grub. Don't think he'd mind."

"The hell with that," Ed protested immediately. "I've got some business to look after. Been gone too long now."

"You reckon this bird — Dagget, or whatever his name is — can ride?" Dave asked.

"Reckon he'll just have to," Ed stated in a flat sort of way. "He's the main reason we're here in the first place."

"Setting in a saddle, ain't that apt to start him to bleeding again?" the cowboy wondered. "I recollect when I —"

"Let it. I ain't going to worry about him."

"Anyway, he'd be doing the town a big

favor if he'd cash in," Dave commented. "Come on, let's get started."

Brinkman moved to Dagget's side, reached down, and took him by his uninjured arm.

"Think you can stand a ride back to Solitude?" he asked, helping Cole to rise.

"Looks like I've got no choices," Cole said wryly. "Just in case I can't, I want you to know what I've said was the gospel truth. I'm no outlaw. I had nothing to do with that holdup. I only wanted my money back — and to help the girl."

Brinkman nodded slightly. "I'm inclined to believe you."

"Appreciate that — seems you're the only one who does. But there's proof that what I say is true. Soon as the Clancy girl regains consciousness you can ask her about it. She'll back what I've said."

Brinkman paused and looked solemnly at Dagget. "Afraid you'd better not depend on her. I doubt if she'll live till she gets to town."

CHAPTER 21

"What'll we do with the stiff?" the man named Ed asked, shifting his attention to the lifeless shape of Cooter sprawled out on the cabin's floor. "I ain't in much of a mind to dig a grave."

"We won't," Brinkman said. "We'll load him across his saddle and tie him down."

"You mean take him back to town? Why the hell bother?" Dave said. "He deserves the same treatment them other two got."

"I'm thinking about the reward that's probably on him," Brinkman explained. "Pretty sure Lester's widow could use the cash."

"Hadn't thought of that!" Ed said, nodding approvingly. "Nobody ever accused Aaron Plummer of overpaying his hired help . . . Give me a hand here, Pete. We'll tote Mister Cooter out and hang him across his horse." The cowboy crossed the room with Ed, and together they took up the outlaw's body and carried it outside.

"Too bad we didn't think to have Wilk and Ben Fontane carry them other two back to town instead of burying them. Probably rewards on them too," Dave said in a regretful tone. Glancing at Dagget, he asked, "You got a price on your head?"

Cole shrugged. "Sorry to disappoint you. Only trouble I've ever had with the law is getting drunk and disturbing the peace."

"Figured you'd say that," Dave said, "but I reckon we'll find out for sure when we talk to the sheriff at Silvertown."

"We got him cinched down," Ed said, coming through the doorway. "Can move out anytime . . . What about Dagget? You want him tied to the saddle, too?"

Brinkman shrugged and looked off across the clearing. "Use your own judgment. Seems hardly necessary."

"Well, I think we will anyway," the bearded Ed murmured, and reaching out took Cole by the arm. "Come on, hard case, aim to tie you down just in case you get the notion to make a run for it."

"Not about to do that," Cole said as he was pushed toward the doorway. "First off, I'm not guilty of anything so I'm not going to give you an excuse to shoot me in the back. Second — I want to get the doctor to fix me up so's I can go on my way, take care of my business."

Dagget limped out into the open and, with Ed still grasping his arm firmly, walked to where his buckskin was standing.

"Climb aboard," Ed directed.

Dagget, taking hold of the saddle horn, swung slowly and painfully up onto the horse. The move sent pain surging through him in solid waves, but he made no sound. It would do him no good, he knew; the best thing was to grit his teeth and keep his mouth shut until they reached town — hoping all the while that Seela Clancy would be in a condition to clear him.

If not, if she were dead or unable to speak, he would be facing a serious problem — a thought he'd had earlier when Harry Brinkman had advised him of the girl's condition. Just how he'd go about proving his innocence Cole did not know, but he'd think of something — he had to. Silent, he watched Ed secure his hands to the gullet of the saddle, then step back.

"Can't see no use of tying his feet together," Dave said, as he and Brinkman came into the open. "He sure ain't in no shape to go nowhere — even if he got loose."

"That's for certain," Ed said. "Anyways, I aim to be riding right behind him, and if he tries anything cute, I'm putting another bullet hole in him. I'm for letting the whole country know that we don't stand for outlaws in Solitude, and that we know what to do with them when we catch them."

Dagget waited quietly, listening to the creak of leather as Ed and the other men turned to their horses and mounted. As he had noted earlier, the sun was out, warm and comforting, and the sky, with the exception of a cluster of dark clouds hanging above the peaks of the Mogollons, had cleared. The world would be a pleasant place at that moment, Cole thought, if he weren't facing so much trouble.

"You going to make it easy and tell us all that you was a partner with them others in that bank robbery?" Dave asked as they moved out in a line for the trail.

Pete and Harry Brinkman were in the lead with the pinto carrying Cooter's body trailing the cowboy at the end of a short rope. Behind the paint horse came Dave riding at the side of Dagget while Ed, puffing contentedly on a curved stem pipe and no more than a length away, brought up the rear.

"I wasn't," Cole said flatly, shaking his head.

With every step of the buckskin, pain ripped through his wounded leg, despite the fact he'd shifted on the saddle and had placed his weight on his stiffened right one. But he reckoned he should figure himself lucky that the bullet striking him had passed through without hitting a bone.

The same held true where his arm was concerned; the bullet had done no great damage as it had bypassed the bone and there was now just a dull throbbing. He could recall little of the slug that had creased his temple. That had simply happened and in less than a wink was over, leaving only the stinging reminder of its passage when later Ed had applied some sort of disinfectant to the raw flesh.

"Ain't no sense in you sticking to that bull," Dave said, taking a plug of dark chewing tobacco from his vest pocket. "We figured it out back there in that cabin where we found you and your partner — and John Clancy's girl."

"What you figured out's all wrong —"

Dave bit off a corner of the plug and laughed. "Sure it is!"

"Plain as day," Ed said from his position slightly behind them. "The four of you robbed the bank — but you wanted it all, even Clancy's girl. And you dang nigh got away with it. You think any judge'll see it otherwise?"

"It's what them lawyer fellows call an open and shut case," Dave said. "You're just going to be wasting time denying it."

"None of it's true," Dagget said shrugging, and winced at the pain the gesture evoked. "The Clancy girl will tell you so soon as she can talk."

Dave spat a stream of brown juice into the weeds growing alongside the trail. "Could be wasting your time there too. That poor kid was hurt bad. None of us figures she'll be alive when John gets her to town — and you're the one responsible for that, you and your dead partner."

"And him being dead, there ain't nothing the law or anybody can do to him for it. Means you'll do your swinging from the gallows all by yourself," Ed said.

Brinkman half turned. "Speakman, why don't you and Conroy leave the man alone!" he snapped. "I'm as tired of hearing your yammering as I expect he is!"

Dagget sighed. He appreciated the rancher's intervention. It was useless trying to convince Ed, whose other name was evidently Speakman, and Dave, who also answered to Conroy, that he was innocent not only where the bank robbery was concerned, but also of kidnapping and later wounding Seela Clancy as well. It would have been one of Cooter's bullets striking the stove and ricocheting that had struck her, but that would be hard to prove.

So far, with the exception of Harry Brinkman, nobody was inclined to listen to him and, in all likelihood, a judge, after hearing them, would turn a deaf ear to his words also. Brinkman seemed to be the only reasonable man he'd encountered so far, but even he, despite the fact he was an influential person in and around Solitude, would be unable to make a stand against the entire town, assuming he desired to do so.

It was a bit of hard luck the two drifters he'd met on the flat, where he'd caught up with Fowler and Apache Reed along with Cooter and Seela Clancy, had not run into the posse. If they'd relayed the message he'd asked them to deliver, it might help to some extent. But, evidently the pair had failed to cross trails with the posse — either by design or accident.

They rode on as the day grew older. Despite the continuing pain, Dagget slept a bit in the saddle, as did the other men. They had been on their horses for many hours and weariness hung on them like a leaden weight. Had his hands not been tied to the saddle, he might have made an attempt to escape, Cole thought at one time, and then immediately dismissed the idea from his mind. To have done so would have turned him immediately into a wanted criminal with lawmen looking for him wherever he went, and Dagget wanted none of that. He was accustomed to being a free man with the choice of going anywhere he wished — and that was the way he'd keep it. Besides, to run for it would be considered an admission of guilt, and he was guilty of nothing.

Late in the afternoon, with the sun streaking the western sky with red-and-gold flame, they pulled off the trail to a small clearing to have a bite to eat. As they drew up, all dismounted except Dagget who remained anchored to his saddle. Seeing this, Harry Brinkman produced his knife and stepped up close to the buckskin.

"All a lot of damn foolishness, tying you down like this," he said, and slashed the bit of rawhide cord Speakman had used. The rancher's tone was impatient. "Man shot up like you are would never get far even if he wanted to."

Speakman and the others made no comment but built a fire and began pooling what food they had left in their grub sacks.

"Help yourself to what's in my saddle-bags," Speakman told Pete. "Don't think there's much but let's use it."

Dave Conroy looked up as the cowboy began to dig into the leather pouches on the buckskin. "Water for coffee's what we're needing. You got any in that canteen?"

Evidently the members of the posse had all neglected to refill their containers when they had the opportunity. Cole, holding his wounded arm and limping over to a log where he could sit down, nodded.

"It's near full," he said, and gestured to Brinkman, who was close by. "Obliged to you for cutting me loose. Made it a bit hard to ride."

Brinkman was in poor humor and showed it. "Was no need for it," he said as he moved off.

They made a meal of beans, salt pork, bread, coffee, and other odds and ends that turned up in the men's saddlebags. When they had finished, they rested for an hour, and then in darkness climbed back into the saddle and resumed the journey to Solitude.

Ed Speakman and Dave Conroy, chastened by Brinkman's sharp tongue, held their peace, and no more words were spoken by them either to Cole or each other — a silence for which Dagget was grateful to the rancher. He would like to think that Brinkman would be his friend and ally once they reached town, but he feared that was too much to hope for. The rancher was interested only in seeing that he got a square deal; he would be on his own insofar as proving his innocence was concerned.

CHAPTER 22

"We don't want to draw no attention when we get to town," Harry Brinkman said as they approached the upper end of Solitude's lone street. "There'll be time enough in the morning for trouble."

It was near midnight. The only lights burning were in the saloons where the music of a piano or a violin mixed with occasional bursts of laughter drifted faintly through the open doorways.

"What'll I do with the dead man?" Pete asked as they turned onto the dusty way. "He'll go to stinking in a few more hours."

"Take him on to the livery stable and turn him over to Counterman — then come back to the jail. May need you," the rancher replied.

"Ain't Counterman likely to be home sleeping?"

"He's got himself a room there in the stable next to the one where he does his undertaking," Conroy said. "Just pound on the door, he'll hear you."

The cowboy turned off into the pale moonlight and angled toward Bell's Livery Stable. Keeping to the shadowy side of the street, Brinkman and the posse continued on toward its farther end.

"If we can get past the saloons, we'll be all right," he murmured. "Sure don't want to argue with a lynching party tonight."

"Where we taking Dagget?" Speakman asked.

"No place around here safe to put him in except the jail."

"Hell, it ain't nothing more than a cracker box. Anybody wanting to can bust in the door."

"The cell's plenty strong. If somebody does break in, he'll still be safe in there behind bars . . . Dave, go rustle up Doc Welch — do it quiet so's nobody'll know what's going on — and tell him to get over here to the jail. Warn him to keep it quiet."

Conroy swung away and headed for the small frame house at the edge of town where the physician lived.

"Seems to me we're going to a hell of a lot of trouble for this — this killer," Speakman grumbled. "Far as I'm concerned, we can turn him over to a lynching party right

214

now and get it over with."

"No," Brinkman said firmly as they rode quietly by the Nugget, keeping well clear of the light rectangle spilling out its open doorway. "The man deserves a fair trial."

"Sure don't agree with you there, Harry. He killed four times — five, if the Clancy girl didn't make it."

"That's how you see it, but maybe it ain't that way. And it's that bit of doubt that makes it necessary that every man gets a fair shake from the law."

Dagget had listened in silence as they continued along the deserted street. He was lucky Harry Brinkman was taking a hand in the matter. The onetime miner and now rancher was the only man who considered the possibility of his being innocent. But that, of course, could end. Brinkman apparently was basing his stand on fair play, and that could end unless he could come up with proof of his innocence, Dagget realized.

And perhaps Brinkman did think him guilty and was holding out against the others only to go through the motions of holding a trial for the sake of establishing Solitude as a good, law-abiding community. If the Clancy girl was unable to talk, or dead, where then could he get the proof that he was not one of the outlaw gang? And failing to do that he certainly would stand no chance before a judge who would believe the story of the bank robbery and abduction just as the posse members had outlined it to him.

The door of the jail was ajar as they rode up to the hitchrack fronting it. One by one, they dismounted, stiff and sore; Dagget came down last of all. His leg and arm had long since settled into a dull throbbing punctuated now and then by knifelike stabs when the buckskin had stumbled or made a misstep for some reason.

"Looks like some damned drifters' been using the place for a hotel again," Speakman said as he opened the door. "Hold up a bit till I get a lamp lit."

Dagget, standing near Harry Brinkman, his face dark and almost obscured by the shadow of his flat-brimmed hat, took a step closer to the rancher. "Obliged to you for standing up for me. I only say that everything I've told you is true. I can prove it if the Clancy girl can talk."

Brinkman, his rugged, hard-cornered features stolid as he waited for Speakman to call out, nodded slightly. "Any man gets a fair trial around here if I have anything to do with it. As for the Clancy girl — Lorena's daughter — just keep hoping she's alive. If she's not, is there any other way you can prove you wasn't one of that outlaw bunch?"

Cole Dagget shrugged. "Not that I can think of right off hand —"

"Well, best you come up with something. John and Lorena Clancy've got a lot of friends in this town who'll listen to them — and do what they want."

"I'm a horse dealer. Can prove that by getting in touch with some of the folks I've sold stock to."

"That'd take a lot of time, and I ain't so sure you've got much. Fact is, the way I expect this town to be feeling, I doubt if I can talk them into taking you to Silvertown and going up before a judge there."

"Meaning —"

"They'll be out to hold a lynching party . . . Let's get off the street. Ed's got the lamp lit."

Dagget, limping badly and favoring his right arm, moved toward the door of the jail with Brinkman a step behind. Speakman was waiting just inside, a gun in one hand, a large ring with a single bronze key in the other.

"Drifters've been holing up here, all right," he said as Cole and the rancher entered. "One of them had the gall to build a fire in that corner over there. Damn wonder the whole place didn't go up in flames. Cell's open," he added, ducking his head in the direction of the adjoining room.

Cole glanced about. The jail, at least the part of it that served as an office for a lawman when the town had one, was almost bare. A single chair placed behind a scarred table that served as a desk was placed near the north wall, a crude bench against the one opposite supplied seats, and there was nothing on the walls or shelves to indicate the room had ever been in use.

"Drifters have either stole or burned up just about everything they could pry loose," Speakman said. "Ought to be a way we could keep this place locked up so's none of them could get in."

Cole felt Brinkman's fingers close gently about his uninjured arm and start him toward the cell in the adjoining room.

"You ain't going to find it very comfortable in there," the rancher said, "but leastwise you'll be safe."

The cell was a six-foot square of bars and a hinged door. A single, small, dirt-streaked window was high in one of the solid rock walls, and inside the cage dust lay an inch deep on the cot and floor. If there had ever been a mat or any blankets, they were missing now — no doubt appropriated by some passing wanderer.

"I'll get your bedroll off your horse," Brinkman said. "Maybe that'll make it a bit more comfortable for you." He paused, glancing toward the outer door.

Dave Conroy, in company with a small, bewhiskered man who barely came up to his shoulder, came into the room. The town's physician, dressed in a shapeless gray suit, with steel-rimmed spectacles on his nose, and carrying a scuffed, black satchel, bustled into the cell where Dagget had sat down on the cot.

"What's the trouble here?" the medical man asked briskly. "Gunshot wound, I suppose."

"Right, Doc," Brinkman said. "Speakman patched him best he could back up the trail."

"Could've done better," the physician grunted, beginning to remove the improvised bandage from Dagget's arm. "Got you in the leg, too, I see — and alongside the head. Son, when you going to learn that flesh and bone can't stop a bullet!"

Brinkman, leaning against the bars of the cell, nodded to Cole. "Expect you know it by now, but this is Doc Welch. Doc, your patient is —"

"I know who he is," Welch snapped, digging into his medicine bag. "He's the fellow that's mixed up in robbing the bank and killing off several men. Don't make much sense me fixing him up so's you can lynch him. Waste of my time."

"Who say's he's going to be lynched?" Brinkman asked, frowning.

"Talk of the whole town ever since John Clancy rode in."

"John's jumping to conclusions. Nobody's proved Dagget guilty of anything but being here at the time it all happened," Brinkman said wearily. "When the hell's this town going to start acting civilized and not like some mining camp run by a miner's court? . . . Get Dagget's blanket roll off his buckskin, Dave, and bring it in here. He'll be needing —"

"What I'm needing is something to put on this cot," Welch said looking up. "I can't treat the man until there's something clean for him to lie on, otherwise he'll die of mortification."

Moving unhurriedly, Conroy crossed to the doorway and stepped out into the cool, starlight-filled night. Several minutes later, while Welch fussed and fumed over the bandages Speakman had wrapped about Dagget's wounds, he reappeared with Cole's blanket roll. Pete, having completed his errand, was at his heels.

"Going to need some hot water," Welch said as Conroy dropped the roll on the cot beside Dagget. "One of you get busy and get a fire started in that stove."

Cole had been waiting for an opportunity to ask the medical man about Seela Clancy. "Doc, what about —"

"Ain't nothing around here to heat water in," Speakman interrupted. "Everything's been stole by them drifters."

"There's a lard tin in my saddlebags that I use for coffee," Dagget said. "Canteen's about half full, too . . . Doc, what about —"

"Then all we're needing is the fire," Welch said impatiently. "Get busy at it. This man's gone too long now. He's lost a lot of blood. I'm surprised he hasn't gone into shock. Good thing he's healthy as a horse otherwise he would have."

"But he's pretty bad, that it, Doc?" Brinkman said.

"Told you he was!" Welch snapped, and got to his feet. He had taken Dagget's bedroll apart and stretched one of the wool blankets over the dust-covered cot. "Guess this'll have to do. How's that water coming?"

Cole, lying full length, was beginning to

feel the effects of his wounds at last. He felt weak and his head throbbed as if it had an Apache war drum going inside it.

"When did you eat last?" Welch asked.

"About dark —"

"Was on the trail coming back," Brinkman added.

"Get him something," the physician said in his abrupt, unyielding way. "Meat, potatoes — plenty of coffee. Go to the back door of the Bluebird. You can raise that dishwasher, or maybe even Lorena."

"I'll go," Brinkman volunteered, and turned to leave. "I don't think anybody else knows he's here, Luther, but maybe we best shut the cell door and lock it, just in case."

The physician nodded and watched as Brinkman closed the heavy grille, locked it, and handed the key through the bars to him.

"I'll be back soon as I can," the rancher said, and halted just inside the doorway. Pete, carrying Cole's canteen and lard tin, brushed by him. "Give that stuff to Doc, Pete, then go down to the Nugget and see if any of the crew's there. Might take a look in the other saloons, too. If you find any of them, send them up here to the jail. We may need some help come morning."

"Sure," the cowhand said, and moved into the cell room where he handed over the water and tin to the medical man.

As Pete hurried off, his hard-heel boots rapping loudly on the bare floor, Welch looked impatiently toward the office area where Conroy and Speakman were working with the stove.

"What the devil's holding up that fire? Water won't be no good to me unless it's boiling. Here's the can and a canteen — come get it." Passing it to Conroy who abandoned the stove briefly, the physician turned to Dagget. "You're shot up some, boy — I expect you know that, but I've seen worse. You'll pull through, although maybe that's not what you want."

"You can bet it is," Dagget said. "Doc, I've been trying to ask you ever since you got here, what about the Clancy girl? Is she going to be all right?"

Welch, laying out clean bandages along with a bottle of antiseptic and a jar of salve on the cot beside Cole, paused.

"Not sure I can give you a good answer to that. The bullet hit her in the head — and then having to make that long ride down the mountain didn't help."

"You think she'll live? Got to know, Doc — it's real important to me."

Luther Welch stood for a time staring through the open doorway into the silvered night. He shook his head.

"I wouldn't plan on it, son," he said.

CHAPTER 23

Dagget awoke shortly before sunrise that next morning. He sat up on the hard cot, his movements painful, and gazed off through the open doorway at the brilliant flare of color in the sky beyond the Mogollons and the more distant Black Range. A grim thought entered his mind; he just could be looking at his last sunrise.

Coming slowly to his feet, Dagget shrugged. If this was the way it was all to end — swinging from the end of a rope for something he did not do — then so be it. He had done his best to make the persons involved believe that he was innocent — and he could, if only they would hold off until Seela Clancy regained consciousness and could speak.

But the temper of the town was high and anger was burning bright in everyone's mind. He had gathered that from hearing talk among the members of the posse, and from what Doc Welch had told Brinkman.

"Reckon our jailbird's up and around," a voice said from the adjoining room.

Cole walked stiffly to the end of the cell. He felt much better than he had the previous night — the ministrations of Luther Welch and the good meal Harry Brinkman had rustled up for him, along with the few hours' sleep, had done wonders for him.

"Howdy," one of the two men standing in the connecting room greeted him. "You're looking a mite peaked."

Both men were dressed in range clothes and were probably range hands working for Brinkman. He shook his head. "Can say I've had better days. You been out there all night?"

"Sure have," the older of the pair, a lean, narrow-faced man with a sweeping mustache, said. "Mr. Brinkman was afeared some of the town's good folks might get a notion to pay you a visit — with a rope. Put me and Fargo to ride herd over you."

The one called Fargo yawned and stretched. He had a round, sunburned face and dark hair and eyes. The open collar of his plaid shirt revealed a long scar running diagonally down his neck.

"I'm obliged to you and Brinkman," Cole said. "Did anybody with a rope show up?"

Fargo grinned. "Nope. Reckon me and Slim scared them off. You mind if I ask you something?"

Dagget shook his head. The sun was out completely now, its rays touching the high peaks and beginning to slowly work their way down into the canyons and onto the flats.

"Give you an answer if I can —"

"Well, I ain't meaning no offense, but did you really shoot up all them fellows the posse claims you did. I'm a mite —"

"Hell, Fargo," Slim cut in, "it ain't fitting to ask a man a question like that!"

Dagget shrugged. "I'm not hiding it. All three were outlaws, and it was either them or me."

"Had a hunch that was the how of it," Fargo said. "Mr. Brinkman ain't the kind to go taking up for owl hoots and rustlers. You had to be all right for him —"

Fargo broke off and, moving up to the outer doorway, stepped out into the open. Looking back over his shoulder, he said, "Well, they're a-coming."

Cole could not see much of the street from his cell, was forced to rely on Fargo and Slim, who were watching the party approaching the jail.

"About two dozen of them," Fargo said.

"One in the middle's carrying a rope."

Slim swore softly. "Expect we're about to start earning our wages," he muttered, and hitched his gun belt. Coming back into the room, he added, "Come on, Fargo, we best get ready for them."

Dagget felt his nerves tighten and a prickling along his scalp. The town's self-appointed judge and jury committee wasn't wasting any time.

"I want you two out of here — gone," Dagget said. "No use of you mixing into it. Useless."

"Well now, I reckon old Fargo and me can hold them off — leastwise for a spell —"

"Just what I'm talking about. You won't be able to stand them off for long."

Fargo scrubbed at his chin. "You ain't meaning that you're just giving up, aiming to let them counterjumpers go right ahead and string you up, are you?"

"Hell no! Last thing I want is to find myself swinging by the neck from a tree somewhere! Just that I aim to do some talking, to prove that I'm who I say I am, and that I'm not an outlaw. The Clancy girl can clear me if she comes to and talks — if not I'll try to figure something else."

"From what I hear, she's in mighty bad shape — bullet right in her head. They're bringing the doc up from Silvertown to see if he can do anything."

"I feel real sorry for her," Cole said. "Was an accident. Bullet glanced off the stove, I figure, and hit her. Is why I'm telling you to get out. If that bunch is dead set on stringing me up, they'll do it. You'll only get yourself killed for nothing trying to stop them."

"But, Mr. Brinkman —"

"I appreciate what he's done for me, but the way the cards are stacked, there's nothing he can do either. Tell him that in case I don't get the chance."

Slim pulled off his hat and ran his bony fingers through his sparse hair. "One thing I'll sure say, you're mighty cool for a man looking at a rope around his neck."

"Maybe not as calm inside as you think. I'm no more anxious to get strung up than the next man, but when you're caught between a rock and a hard place there's not much left to do but to take what's coming. I sure don't plan on letting that bunch see me beg."

"I can savvy that," Fargo said. "Now, you sure there ain't nothing me and Slim can do. They're about here."

"No, and I'm obliged to you both. Just you stand back and let them have their way."

"What'll we tell Mr. Brinkman when he shows up? He had to ride out to the ranch and said he'd be back here early."

"Just that this is the way I wanted it," Cole said. "Now open up this cell and let me out."

Fargo produced the key, turned the lock, and allowed the barred grille to swing open. His nerves taut, and the tingling along his scalp more pronounced, Cole nodded to the two men, crossed into the outer office, and moved into the street.

The advancing men halted briefly, and then came on. A coolness belying the turmoil within him settled over Cole Dagget. Arms at his sides, he waited. John Clancy was one of those in the lead. The man beside him carrying the rope was a stranger. Elsewhere among the lynch mob, he spotted Ed Speakman and Dave Conroy. There were no other familiar faces.

The party halted again, this time only a few strides in front of Dagget. Some of the men held rifles in their hands, others were wearing six-guns. All were eyeing Slim and Fargo warily. Dagget took note of the fact.

"They won't give you any trouble," he called out. "Want you to leave them out of it."

"You just coming peaceable along, that

it?" Clancy asked. It was apparent that he had no sleep. His face was haggard and there was a dullness in his eyes.

"Don't see that I have any choice," Cole said quietly, "but I aim to have my say first. You're wrong — and you're making a mistake. I —"

"That's not the way we see it or what we've been told," a man in the front of the mob yelled. "What you done's plain as the nose on your face — and around here, a killing calls for a hanging! Come on — let's take him down to the Nugget. That big cottonwood growing alongside it'll do just fine for what we've got to do. Somebody best tie his hands."

Yells of approval sounded in the cool, early morning air. Clancy and another man seized Dagget by the arms and held him while a third bound his wrists together. That done, they jerked him roughly about and headed back up the street. As the party marched along, others coming on the scene yelled questions and then joined in; and by the time they reached the huge cottonwood that spread its branches over the Nugget and the open ground to the south of it, the crowd had grown to twice its original size.

Taut, the knowledge that death was only minutes away filling his mind, Cole Dagget glanced around. Everyone living in Solitude was probably present, he thought, and the two soldiers he could see riding in from the south would also be there to take in the enjoyment that people seemed to get from watching a lynching. He glanced to his left. The man with the rope, hanging tight to one end, threw the coil over a limb extending at a right angle from the tree's trunk. Catching the dangling noose, he wheeled to the crowd.

"Get a horse over here for him to set on while I tie the rope to that post there."

Two men immediately separated from the party and trotted toward several horses picketed behind the saloon. In only moments, with their ruddy features shining with sweat, despite the coolness of the early hour, they returned.

"Here you are, Kebro," one said.

Kebro, when the end of the rope was secured to a post, took the reins offered and led the horse back to where Dagget, his hands tied, stood between John Clancy and another man. Opening the noose, he dropped it around Cole's neck.

"I reckon this'll let folks know we don't put up with outlaws and killers around here," he said, looking out over the now silent crowd.

"What you'll be letting them know is that you're all a bunch of murderers," Dagget said coldly.

"The hell! Wasn't any of us that shot down poor old Lester Zale or put a bullet in the Clancy girl's head."

"Wasn't me either — told you that. And I'm telling you again, I'm not one of the outlaws."

"You swear to God on that?" a voice in the crowd called out. "Can you prove it?"

"I swear it — and I can prove it if you'll give me time."

"Don't listen to him, George," Clancy said loudly. "We done heard all this back up the trail when we caught him. Ain't a bit of truth in it."

The man named George, another miner from the looks of his clothes, shook his head. "Sure can't see that there's all this big hurry — and I'd hate to think I'd had a hand in hanging the wrong man."

"He's the right man — ain't no doubt of that," Clancy said.

"If you want proof that I'm not, go talk to your daughter," Cole said, putting his attention on Clancy. "She'll tell you I'm not one of the outlaws, that I tried to help her."

Clancy lowered his head. "The girl's still

unconscious. She couldn't tell you nothing."

"Then get in touch with the commanders or the supply officers at Fort Bayard, or Wingate, or Union. They'll identify me — I've sold them horses. There are some other forts, too, that I've done business with —"

Ed Speakman took a step forward from his place in the front of the line. "Man's stalling, that's all he's doing. Knows we'd have to send somebody to Silvertown where there's a telegraph. Probably be a waste of time."

"Then talk to the banker here. He'll tell you that I was in the bank cashing a draft for a bunch of horses I'd sold —"

"Banker ain't here — went to Silvertown yesterday to make a report on the robbery and won't be back till sometime today, or even tomorrow."

"Don't mean nothing anyway," Clancy said. "You probably killed some poor sucker and took that draft off him. Or maybe you stole the horses and sold them to the Army."

Dagget, frustration, anger, and desperation all coursing through him, swore deeply. He was failing to get anywhere with the crowd. Someone had an answer for everything he said — but that was the way with a lynching party he'd heard. There was no reasoning with the men in a mob bent on exacting what they believed to be justice.

"Send a telegram to Tom Lockhart. He's got a big ranch near Fort Worth in Texas. He'll tell you who I am. Fact is, I'm marrying his daughter."

"Reckon she's a widow before she'll even be a bride," someone said with a laugh.

"Can't send no telegram from here. Have to go to Silvertown," Clancy said. "If you —"

The sound of horses coming up fast brought everyone around. It was Harry Brinkman and a number of his crew. Hope lifted within Dagget. Maybe the rancher could persuade Clancy and the crowd to wait until he could produce proof that he was who he claimed to be.

"It's Brinkman," someone said unnecessarily. "Figured he'd be showing up and putting in his two cents' worth."

The rancher and the men with him, riding abreast as they came up the street, slowed briefly while Fargo and Slim joined them. Cole watched as the pair moved in close to Brinkman, said a few words, and then took their places in the line that extended the width of the street. Reaching the crowd, they halted, the nervous hooves of their horses stirring up clouds of dust.

"Stay out of this, Brinkman!" Clancy warned as the rancher dismounted. "Damned killer's going to get what he's got coming to him."

"I'm not for certain he's got anything coming to him," Brinkman said coldly. "You're not sure he's guilty — and neither is anybody else around here."

"There's enough proof for me. My girl's laying —"

"Not enough proof to satisfy the law. When the hell are we going to stop acting like vigilantes and going off half-cocked every time something like this happens?"

"You saying he ain't guilty?" the man called George asked.

"I don't know much more about it than you do, but I've been doing a lot of thinking about it and I've got my doubts. Point is, the man's entitled to a fair trial before a judge and where he can tell his side of it."

Clancy shook his head and glanced about. The crowd had increased some and there were now several women present.

"He keeps saying he didn't do anything wrong," someone in the mob said, "but he ain't never proved it. All he does is talk about it."

"Yeah, saying that there's army officers at the forts that'll back him, and some rancher way over in Texas. Ain't nothing he can tie onto around here."

"Won't be hard to find out if he's lying about that," Brinkman said. "Let's take him to Silvertown and send telegrams to these people he's talking about. There's a judge there too —"

"I'm against that," Ed Speakman said. "This here outlaw is our problem and we ought to keep it that way. Besides what he's offering as proof that he ain't one of the outlaws won't hold water there no more'n it will here."

"Then we can at least wait until Seela Clancy has regained consciousness and can talk. She was with that bunch. She knows which side Dagget here was on," Brinkman said.

"Afraid the girl won't be able to help him," Welch said, moving up from the street to the edge of the crowd. "I was waiting for the doctor in Silvertown to come, but the girl took a turn for the worse. Had to go ahead and take the bullet out of her brain myself —"

"Is she dead?" Clancy asked in a strained voice.

"No, John, she's still alive, but just barely. But I can't say that means much. Way it looks to me, she'll never wake up — just be unconscious for the rest of her life."

CHAPTER 24

Cole Dagget felt a heaviness settle through him. Seela Clancy was the same as dead. Not only was it a sad happening, but it meant that his best hope for proving his innocence was gone.

"Get him on that horse!" a voice shouted, abruptly breaking the silence.

"String him up — that's what he's got coming!" another took up the cry for vengeance.

Cole felt the crowd close in about him. Hands seized his arms, sending jagged pain shooting through him. Someone crowded up hard against his leg, heightening the pain there also. He glanced out over the crowd to the angry faces, to the two soldiers talking with someone at the edge of the milling mob, to the deserted, dusty street beyond.

This was the way it was all going to wind up for him, he thought bitterly — dangling from the end of a rope for something he didn't do. All his hopes, his plans for a life with Beth, a horse ranch — all gone in the blowing dust. Why —

A gunshot blasted through the noisy confusion. Cole felt the fingers gripping his arms relax and the men nearby come to a halt. Abruptly, Harry Brinkman, shouldering his way through the crowd, appeared. Farther back, the members of his crew, still mounted, guns drawn, were looking on, their browned, hard-cornered faces impassive.

"I'm not letting this happen!" Brinkman said in a loud voice. "This man's going to get a fair trial or —"

"The hell with you!" John Clancy shouted, pushing up to confront the rancher. "You keep out of this!" he added, and swung a rock-hard fist at the rancher.

The blow caught Brinkman on the side of the head, sent him staggering back into the man behind him, but he didn't go down. Recovering immediately, he surged forward. Hands knotted into fists, he drove a left into Clancy's face, followed with a right that sent his onetime partner reeling to one side.

The crowd, filling the air with yells, had pulled back to form a circle, but the line of riders from Brinkman's ranch had not moved and remained where they were despite their fidgeting horses, turned restless by the shouting and the scuffling about of the two men.

"You been asking for this ever since me and Lorena got married!" Cole heard Clancy shout. "You just never got over her picking me instead of you."

In the next instant, Clancy rushed in. Head down, he charged Brinkman. The rancher sidestepped, avoided the miner's wildly swinging fists, and smashed a sharp blow to Clancy's unprotected jaw. Brinkman's mouth was pulled down into a hard, satisfied sort of grin as if he were welcoming the encounter.

Clancy wheeled, came back fast. His arms were no longer swinging, but outstretched as he sought to wrap Harry Brinkman in a powerful bear hug. The rancher jerked away, but not fast enough. Clancy's thick arms encircled him, and locked together the two men began to wrestle back and forth.

Brinkman, his own arms clamped to his sides, tripped and both went down. The fall broke Clancy's grip on the rancher, allowed him to roll away and come to his feet. Plastered with dust, muttering curses, Clancy scrambled upright too and, face contorted with fury, lowered his head once more and rushed straight at Brinkman.

With the same grim smile of satisfaction pulling at his lips, the rancher settled himself squarely on his booted feet and, with fists poised, waited. As Clancy closed in, Brinkman met him with an uppercut that cracked like a whip when it connected with Clancy's jaw. The miner's head snapped up and his eyes rolled back. Brinkman swung again, drove a hard right to his old friend's head, followed with a left again to the chin. Clancy staggered back. Flat-footed, with arms hanging loosely at his sides, he began to sway uncertainly. At once Brinkman stepped in close, and catching the man by the shoulders, kept him from falling. Turning about then, he pushed Clancy into the arms of Speakman.

"Look after him, Ed," he said between heavy breaths, and coming around, he moved up to where Dagget was standing. Removing the noose from around Cole's neck, he took out his knife and cut the cord binding his wrists together.

"I'm taking this man out to my ranch," he said to the crowd in general. "Aim to keep him there until we can get a judge up here that'll hold a proper trial — like civilized folks are supposed to do. Now, if any of you've got any ideas about coming out after him, I won't be responsible for what will happen."

"Are you Cole Dagget?"

At the question, Cole turned. One of the soldiers he had noticed riding in earlier faced him. "That's me."

"I'm Lieutenant John Roth. Man with me is Private Gilman. We're from Fort Wingate."

Dagget frowned. Wingate was a good customer. "There something wrong?"

On beyond the crowd, two more riders had entered the street, one heading up to the hitchrack at Lorena Clancy's Bluebird Café, the other, Plummer, the banker, continuing along the way. The dust raised by Brinkman and Clancy still hung in the warm air, and somewhere back among the houses a rooster was crowing belatedly.

"No, sir, nothing's wrong far as we're concerned," Roth replied, glancing suggestively at the rope still dangling from the cottonwood, "but I'm not sure about you."

"That's settled for the moment," Dagget said. "What do you want with me?"

"I've got an order here from Captain Groves. Expect you know him — he's in charge of the horses."

Cole nodded. John Clancy, in company with a dozen or more of the crowd were hurrying toward the Bluebird. Evidently the man who had ridden in with Aaron Plummer was the long-awaited doctor from Silvertown.

"I know the captain —"

"I've brought an order from him for twenty more horses. We're expecting a new batch of recruits and we'll need mounts for them. Sent me after you — said I might have to chase you to a place called Mangas Springs, but to keep going until I did. Lucky I caught up with you here — and just in time," the officer said, again looking at the rope.

"You know this man?" Brinkman asked, voicing his question in a loud voice.

"Not personally, but I've seen him around the post," Roth replied. "Been supplying horses to us and the other forts around here for quite a spell. Supply officers like to deal with him because his stock's always the best . . . Were you about to hang him?"

"Lynch him," Brinkman said. "There was a bank robbery and a kidnapping. Lot of folks thought he was in on it."

"Him an outlaw?" Roth said, shaking his head. "I sure doubt that, mister. Somebody's made a mistake. He's too busy selling horses to the Army to be an outlaw."

Brinkman looked out over the crowd. "You all hear that? You need any more proof that what Dagget said was true?"

"Enough for me," someone answered. His words were followed by a chorus of accord.

"Then I reckon you're free to go," the rancher said, nodding at Cole. "Where's your horse?"

"In the stable, I guess."

"Go get it for him, Jess," Brinkman said, motioning to a member of his crew. And then to Cole, "You're welcome to come stay at my place till you get to feeling better."

"Obliged to you, but I've got to move on. Was due at Mangas Springs a couple of days ago — horse deal."

"You'll find it mighty hard riding with that leg of yours in the shape it's in."

"I'll manage," Dagget said, and came back to Lieutenant Roth. "Tell the captain I'll have his horses there soon as I can — be less than a month."

"Yes, sir, I'll give him the word — and good luck," the officer said, and began to move away.

"Aaron!" Brinkman called as the crowd started to break up and drift off. "I think you owe this man some money, eight hundred dollars that those outlaws took off him when they robbed you."

Plummer came forward slowly. "Yes, I remember — he was in cashing a draft. Let

me go in, count the money in that sack, and
—"

"No need for that," Dagget said as the cowhand named Jess led up the buckskin. "Got my money. Took it out of the sack when I caught Fowler and Reed. You don't owe me anything."

Brinkman laughed and shook his head. "Now, that's pure, naked honesty! The man could have kept his mouth shut and collected another eight hundred dollars — but he didn't!"

"Guess we were wrong about him all the way," Kebro said, drawing his rope off the Cottonwood's limb. "Sure begging your pardon, Dagget, but Clancy was so dead sure that you was in on it —"

"Could say you'd make one hell of a good lawman!" a man in the crowd declared. "Tracking that bunch down like you done, shooting it out with them, and then getting back all of the bank's money sure was quite a chore! How about taking on the job as our marshal?"

Dagget, accepting the buckskin's reins from Brinkman's crew member, swung stiffly and painfully up into the saddle. A wry smile parted his lips. Only a few minutes earlier, these men had been clamoring for his life, now they were asking him to be

Solitude's lawman.

"Nope, I reckon not," he said. "Like what I'm doing, dealing in horses."

"That what you are — a horse trader?"

The usual denial and explanation rose quickly as always, and then Dagget shrugged. What was the use? Horse dealer or horse trader, no one ever seemed to get it right, and he guessed it really didn't matter. In fact, after what he'd just been through, only the important things now seemed of importance.

"Yeah, that's right," he said, and expressing his thanks to Harry Brinkman again, rode north out of town for Mangas Springs. Maybe he wouldn't be too late.

THE MAN BEHIND THE BOOK

"I appreciate my readers' loyalty. I've tried never to let them down with a second-rate story — and I won't."

No Western author has been more faithful to his fans than Robert Raymond Hogan, a man known as "Mr. Western" by Old West fans in over 100 countries around the world. Since the appearance of *Ex-Marshal* (1956), his first Western novel, Ray Hogan has produced entertaining Western stories of consistent quality and historical significance at a breakneck pace.

This prolific author's credentials rank him among the great Western writers of all time. Hogan's credits include 143 novels and over 225 articles and short stories. His works have been filmed, televised, and translated into nineteen foreign languages.

"I'm a person with a great love for the American West, and respect for the people who developed it. I don't think we give enough

credit to the pioneers who moved west of the Missouri in the early days."

Ray Hogan's ancestors first arrived in America from Northern Ireland in 1810. Commencing with his great-grandfather, who journeyed from Pennsylvania to Kansas around 1825, losing his life to Osage or Pawnee Indians, Hogan family history is one of western migration. His grandfather moved from Tennessee to Missouri, and his father began a law enforcement career as an early Western marshal in the "Show Me" state before moving to New Mexico when Ray was five years old.

The wild frontier of yesterday is simply family to Ray Hogan. His lawman father met and talked with Frank James after the famous outlaw was released from jail, and once suffered a serious stab wound in the chest while bringing a train robber to justice. Ray's wife, Lois Easterday Clayton, is the daughter of a New Mexico family with its own pioneer heritage. Her grandfather began commuting between New Mexico and Missouri by horseback and stage in 1872 as a circuit-riding Methodist preacher "with a rifle across his knees." At one time he encountered the Dalton gang in Missouri.

Ray Hogan's boyhood was spent hunting,

fishing, and riding horses in the New Mexico backcountry, observing all that was said and done on working ranches, and cocking an ear in hotel lobbies while railroad men, rodeo performers, townsmen, and cowhands talked about life on the range. It was only natural that he decided to devote his lifetime to firsthand examination of the Old West.

Ray Hogan is a meticulous researcher, his investigations having taken him all over the West. An extensive personal library of books, pamphlets, maps, pictures, and miscellaneous data attests his ravenous appetite for Western details. Throughout his intense lifelong study he has painstakingly strived for authenticity.

Readers equate a Ray Hogan Western with excellence. His trademark is a good story full of human interest and action, set against a factual Western background.

"I've attempted to capture the courage and bravery of those men and women that lived out West, and the dangers and problems they had to overcome."

Ray Hogan still resides in the Land of Enchantment with his equally talented wife, Lois, an accomplished artist and designer. This outstanding American continues to deliver in a way unsurpassed by his peers, keeping the Old West alive for others born too late.

ABOUT THE AUTHOR

Ray Hogan is an author who has inspired a loyal following over the years since he published his first Western novel *Ex-marshal* in 1956. Hogan was born in Willow Springs, Missouri, where his father was town marshal. At five the Hogan family moved to Albuquerque where Ray Hogan still lives in the foothills of the Sandia and Manzano mountains. His father was on the Albuquerque police force and, in later years, owned the Overland Hotel. It was while listening to his father and other old-timers tell tales from the past that Ray was inspired to recast these tales in fiction. From the beginning he did exhaustive research into the history and the people of the Old West and the walls of his study are lined with various firearms, spurs, pictures, books, and memorabilia, about all of which he can talk in dramatic detail. Among his most popular works are the series of books about Shawn Starbuck, a searcher in a quest for a lost brother, who has a clear sense of right and wrong and who is willing to stand up and be counted when it is a question of fairness or justice. His other major series is about lawman John Rye whose reputation has earned him the sobriquet 'The Doomsday Marshal'. 'I've attempted to capture the courage and bravery of those men and women that lived out West and the dangers and problems they had to overcome,' Hogan once remarked. If his lawmen protagonists seem sometimes larger than life, it is because they are men of integrity, heroes who through grit of character and common sense are able to overcome the obstacles they encounter despite often overwhelming odds. This same grit of character can also be found in Hogan's heroines and, in *The Vengeance of Fortuna West*, Hogan wrote a gripping and totally believable account of a woman who takes up the badge and tracks the men who killed her lawman husband by ambush. No less intriguing in her way is Nellie Dupray, convicted of rustling in *The Glory Trail*. Above all, what is most impressive about Hogan's Western novels is the consistent quality with which each is crafted, the compelling depth of his characters, and his ability to juxtapose the complexities of hu-